Krispin wai...
clicking the O...

He didn't need to sue her. He could let it drop. "I suppose a new kayak would be worth the pain and suffering." He leaned back in the chair.

A gentle knock on the door woke him. It took a few moments to get to his feet and catch his bearings. He went to the door and saw a honey-haired woman with a timid smile on luscious pink lips staring at him. "Hello?"

"Hi, I'm Jess Kearns. I . . ." She looked down at the wooden planks on the small deck. "I'm the one who ran you over."

"Ah." He didn't remember her being this beautiful. Of course he never really got a good view of her. "Come in; you've saved me the trouble of tracking you down."

"Yes, sir. I've brought my insurance information. I hauled the kayak out of the harbor, but it's not repairable."

"I can imagine." He didn't want to be angry with this woman, but he was. "Have a seat."

"No, thank you." She handed him a piece of paper. "Here's all the information you need to know."

He scanned the sheet. "My lawyer will be in touch." He dropped the paper onto the table.

"Lawyer? Won't it be easier just going through the insurance company?"

"I'm planning on suing you, Ms. Kearns. You nearly killed me."

LYNN A. COLEMAN lives in north central Florida with her pastor husband of thirty-two years. She has three grown children and eight grandchildren. She enjoys writing for the Lord. She is the co-founder and founding president of American Christian Fiction Writers, Inc. Currently she is the E-Region director of the Florida Writers Association. Lynn enjoys hearing from her readers. Visit her Web site at www.lynncoleman.com.

Books by Lynn A. Coleman

HEARTSONG PRESENTS
HP314—Sea Escape
HP396—A Time to Embrace
HP425—Mustering Courage
HP443—Lizzy's Hope
HP451—Southern Treasures
HP471—One Man's Honor
HP506—Cords of Love
HP523—Raining Fire
HP574—Lambert's Pride
HP635—Hogtied
HP728—A Place of Her Own
HP762—Photo Op
HP772—Corduroy Road to Love
HP782—Trespassed Hearts

Suited
for Love

Lynn A. Coleman

Heartsong Presents

I'd like to dedicate this book to all eight of my grandchildren: Jonathan, Joshua, Leanna, Serenity, Matthew, Kayla, Jeremiah, and Hannah. God's grace has blessed me with a wonderful husband. Then He blessed us with three children who have turned around and blessed us with the eight of you. My prayer for each of you is that you will find the gift of a spouse who is suited for loving you and Him. God bless you all.

Love, Grandma

A note from the Author:
I love to hear from my readers! You may correspond with me by writing:

Lynn A. Coleman
Author Relations
PO Box 721
Uhrichsville, OH 44683

ISBN 978-1-60260-067-6

SUITED FOR LOVE

All of the characters and events in this book are fictitious. Any resemblance to actual persons, living or dead, or to actual events is purely coincidental.

Our mission is to publish and distribute inspirational products offering exceptional value and biblical encouragement to the masses.

PRINTED IN THE U.S.A.

one

"Stop!" someone screamed.

Crack. The sound of wood scraping underneath Jess's boat hull caused her to frantically search the water from port to starboard. She put the engine in neutral. Pieces of a red kayak slithered past. Arms and the upper body of a man surfaced. Jess jumped overboard. *Dear Lord, have I killed him? Oh God, please help.*

She reached the man and flipped him onto his back. Shifting her body out of the foul-weather gear and losing her boots, she reached across the man's chest and swam with him to the dock. Time was of the essence.

A couple of fishermen joined her at the dock and pulled the limp man out of the water. Jess climbed onto the pier. Immediately she checked his airway and began performing CPR.

"We called the paramedics, Jess," Bill Hayden reported.

Jess counted, inhaled, and blew the fresh air into his mouth. *Please, Lord.* She held back the tears.

She began chest compressions and counted to thirty. Two more breaths, then back to chest compressions. "One, two. . ."

The man sputtered. Saltwater flowed out of his mouth. Jess turned him to his side to allow the water from the man's lungs to continue to pour out. He opened his eyes. They were a rich royal blue with shafts of gray radiating from the pupil.

Jess's hands shook. "I'm sorry. I'm so sorry," she mumbled.

The man coughed.

She rubbed the man's back for a moment, hoping to ease the strain the coughing dealt his body. "Anyone got a blanket?" she called without lifting her eyes. He convulsed. She was shaking. "Dear Lord," she whispered, "please!"

The intensity of the sirens caused Jess to look up toward the street. It was low tide, and the paramedics would have to carry him up fifty steps to reach the ambulance. Seemingly half the town lined Squabbin Bay's rocky cliff harbor, which looked like so many other coastal towns in Maine. A large, meaty hand fell on her shoulder. "He's going to be all right, Jess." The firm, even tones of her father's voice calmed her.

The paramedics made it down the long dock with a body board in tow. As soon as they arrived, she left the stranger in their care. Jess rubbed her face with her cold hands. May was not the time of year to go swimming in the North Atlantic. She trembled—whether from the shock of the accident or the frigid water, it didn't matter. She'd nearly killed a man. How could she have missed a bright red kayak?

"What happened?" Josie Smith asked. Josie had worked for the fire department as a paramedic since before the time Jess fell off the monkey bars at school and needed stitches. At eight, having to ride in the ambulance had been a rather cool experience.

"I don't know. I never saw him until after I heard the boat crunching the hull." Jess shook off the horrible image and sounds that flickered through her mind.

"Jess?" Todd snorted. "You?" Todd was her age. He had gone right from high school to training for the fire department. She and Todd had been rivals for various athletic titles while in grammar school. In high school Jess had discovered her femininity and lost interest in running and climbing ropes— unlike her best friend, Randi, who ran five miles every day, until she was eight months pregnant.

"I didn't see him. I don't know where he came from." She hesitated. As a kid she'd won more awards for water safety than the rest of her friends. "I must not have been paying attention," she mumbled.

Todd grabbed his walkie-talkie and reported the injured

stranger's situation. Jess stepped back. He was out of her hands now. She prayed he would be all right. Her father came alongside, wrapped her in a towel, and pulled her into his embrace just as her stepmother, Dena, arrived at the top of the dock. Dena had been married to Jess's father for the past two years. A lot had happened in that time. Jess had just finished college and moved to Boston, only to discover her job experience didn't bode well with her Down-Eastern ways. The struggle for success meant being less than honest with her coworkers, and that was something Jess couldn't adjust to. So she'd come home and within six months started forming a co-op for the local lobstermen in much the same way that the cranberry farmers had done decades ago.

"What happened?" her father whispered.

"I honestly don't know. I put the boat into a slow approach to the dock and—smack—I ran into him. I didn't see him, Dad. I swear."

"Kayaks are low riding."

Jess scanned the harbor. Another lobsterman was on board her boat, *Jessy*, and bringing it back to the dock. "Did our *Jessy* drift in toward the rocks?"

"Probably scraped a barnacle or two off. Don't fret about it. Do you have a change of clothes on board?"

"Nope."

"Foul-weather gear in the harbor?"

"Yup." She scanned the remains of the red kayak.

The paramedics started to carry the stranger up the long walkway of the floating dock. Due to low tide, it was quite a climb. A few others helped. Jess looked back at the sinking debris of the kayak. *What have I done?*

❧

Krispin moaned and pushed himself up on the recliner. *Of all the stupid things to have happened.* He let out a long gasp of air. Unable to deal with the conflicting emotions between whether to wring his aggressor's neck or hug his savior for her quick thinking, he groaned again. He'd rented this remote cottage in a little-known place to have peace, not to be smashed into pieces.

For the past seven years, he'd been working his way up the corporate ladder. Finally, with a little luck, he'd made it to a senior position in the company. But he felt empty, alone, and couldn't understand why. He had all he ever wanted, and then some, but life wasn't adding up. "Now, this," he muttered and leaned over to pick up the phone.

On the second ring, his secretary answered, giving the usual formal greeting.

"Hi, Amanda, it's me."

"Mr. Black, how are you? How's your vacation?"

"Fine, fine. Actually, no, it isn't fine. I've had an accident. Is Gary in?"

"Yes, sir. Are you all right?"

"Mild concussion," he admitted, but he wouldn't confess to her he was lucky to be alive. The office would have it blown out of proportion by the time he was due back on Monday. . .*three days*. He wouldn't be back by Monday. He knew that before the accident. The injury just gave him a good excuse.

"Krisp, you all right?" Gary seldom showed any real concern for anyone apart from how it would affect business.

"I'll be all right. But the doc said I shouldn't drive for a few days, especially not the long distance back to Manchester from here."

"Gotcha. What happened? And what clients do I need to know about for next week?"

Krispin filled him in. He rubbed his throbbing temples and closed his eyes. "Gary, I hate to do this, but can I call you back later? I'm feeling a little nausea coming on."

"TMI." Gary groaned. "Take another week; we'll cover for you."

"Thanks, I could use it."

"Should I send Maureen up?"

Krispin squeezed his eyes closed. Gary had been trying to set Krispin up with Maureen for ages. He dated her on occasion but only when he had no other option. Maureen was Gary's younger sister. Nice enough gal, but they had nothing in common—except Gary. "No thanks. I'm going to be busy taking care of a lawsuit, I'm sure."

Gary whistled. "Betcha end up owning that boat."

"More than likely." And that's the way it was in his world. Fight until the person next to you drops or you bring him to the poorhouse. But how could he sue her after she saved his life? "Later, Gary."

"Later."

Krispin waited to hear the disconnect before clicking the OFF button of the cordless phone. He didn't need to sue her. He could let it drop. "I suppose a new kayak would be worth the pain and suffering." He leaned back in the chair.

A gentle knock on the door woke him. It took a few moments to get to his feet and catch his bearings. He went to the door and saw a honey-haired woman with a timid smile on luscious pink lips staring at him. "Hello?"

"Hi, I'm Jess Kearns. I . . ." She looked down at the wooden planks on the small deck. "I'm the one who ran you over."

"Ah." He didn't remember her being this beautiful. Of course he never really got a good view of her. "Come in; you've saved me the trouble of tracking you down."

"Yes, sir. I've brought my insurance information. I hauled the kayak out of the harbor, but it's not repairable."

"I can imagine." He didn't want to be angry with this woman, but he was. "Have a seat."

"No, thank you." She handed him a piece of paper. "Here's all the information you need to know."

He scanned the sheet. "My lawyer will be in touch." He dropped the paper onto the table.

"Lawyer? Won't it be easier just going through the insurance company?"

"I'm planning on suing you, Ms. Kearns. You nearly killed me."

Tears filled her eyes. His stomach knotted. *Why'd I say that?*

"I'm sorry. You're welcome to sue me. I don't have much, but anything I have is yours." She scurried past him and out the door.

Krispin stood there for a moment. *How odd. Doesn't she know that she's admitted guilt? No lawyer would have trouble taking her for all she's worth.* "Wait," he called out.

She kept running and then jumped into a red Mercedes convertible.

"She doesn't have anything? Yeah, right!" Krispin reached for the phone to call his lawyer, then paused. *She said I could have it all. Do I want that?*

❧

Jess couldn't believe her ears. The man wanted to sue her. While she didn't own much, she may well have put her father into jeopardy, and possibly Dena. *Dear Lord, protect my parents from my careless actions.*

She fretted the entire drive home. After she told her parents the news, they called their attorney and prepared for the lawsuit. Her father's lobster boat and business were worth a small amount, but Wayne and Dena had previously taken steps to incorporate their various businesses so that if one should fail, they wouldn't lose it all. Five hours later Jess had a computer printout of the worth of the lobster business, her mortgage, a statement of personal worth, another copy of the insurance policy, as well as a statement from the lawyer regarding his contact information. A plastic container of Dena's homemade chicken soup sat on the passenger seat beside her as she drove up to Krispin Black's house for the second time that day.

A faint light glowed in the living room of the rental cottage. Jess used to play here with her girlfriends years ago when Mindy's parents owned the cottage. But like so many others, they had moved farther south and sold the property.

She knocked on the door. No answer. Peering into the living room, she looked for any signs of life. He lay on the recliner with a cup in his hand. She watched his body tense, then relax. The cup dropped to the floor. He didn't respond.

Jess opened the door and walked in. She took his pulse. It seemed steady. His hand suddenly clutched her wrist. "What are you doing here?"

"I. . .I came to bring you the information for the lawsuit."

"What?" He jumped up from his chair, then collapsed.

"Do you have a concussion?"

He nodded his head and groaned.

"Sit back. When was the last time you took your medicine?"

"I don't know." A glazed look clouded his blue eyes.

Jess flipped open her cell phone and called Josie. Within minutes Jess was told what to look for and to give the word if she needed any further help. Josie would be right over.

"Have you eaten?"

"I don't think so."

Jess looked through the small kitchen. A half-eaten, stale bagel sat next to a very cold cup of coffee. "Breakfast," she mumbled. Finding a pot, she heated up the soup and went back to the living room. She looked into his eyes, his incredibly handsome eyes, and swallowed.

"You like?" he purred.

Jess closed her eyes and prayed. She hadn't dealt with a man like this in years. She ignored his question and pushed on. "What day is it?"

"Friday." He glanced out the window. "Possibly Saturday. How late is it?"

"Not that late, Mr. Black. I have some soup heating on the stove. Do you have a wife or someone to watch over you?"

"Nope. You offering?"

"Jesus wouldn't want me to ignore your condition. I'll call my dad and he'll come over."

"Your father? Don't bother. I thought. . ."

"Mr. Black, I'm fairly sure I know what you thought, but I'm not that kind of a girl. I'm sorry you were injured at my hand, but please show me some respect."

Krispin Black scanned her face, then closed his eyes. "You're right. I apologize. It was terribly rude of me."

"Apology accepted. Let me get your soup." She left him and called her father. He couldn't come but would find someone right away. Placing the bowl of warm soup on the dinette, she asked, "Are you able to make it to the table on your own?"

"I think I can manage."

Jess held herself back as she watched the proud man work his way over. They sat in silence as he ate.

"Thank you." He pushed the bowl away. "That was thoughtful."

"You're welcome." She reached for the pile of papers. "Here's all the information you'll need for your lawsuit. Our lawyer's name and contact info is on top."

He scanned the pages. "It's not your boat?"

"No, it's my father's."

"And he's willing to give up on this without a fight?"

She smiled. "I didn't say that. He's hired his attorney. But they knew you'd order to obtain this information, so we just prepared it in advance."

"You're nuts." He paused. "Sorry."

"No, we're not nuts, we're Christians. And I was at fault." She paused for a moment, then looked directly into his eyes. "You don't believe, do you?"

"Nah, never had much use for religion. Didn't see the point. It's all right, I mean. I'm not against it or anything. But if there truly is a God, why would He concern Himself with the likes of me or anyone else in the world?"

Jess smiled. "Because He loves us."

"You really believe all that stuff?"

"Yup."

Krispin gently wagged his head back and forth.

"You can call it my Christian love that brought over these papers and that soup and the friend who's going to spend the night with you to make sure you're okay."

"Why would you do that? I mean, I get the Christian thing, but I told you I was going to sue you." The disbelief was written all over his face.

"Krispin. . ." She paused. A desire to reach out and touch him caught her by surprise. "I honestly did not see you as I was approaching the dock. I must have looked down for a moment and missed your entering the waterway in front of me. I'm just thankful I was able to save you. I don't think I could live with myself knowing I killed a man." She pulled her hands back to her lap. *Lord, what do You have in mind here? Did this accident occur to bring this man to salvation? Your will, Father, not mine.*

"Jess—you did say your name was Jess, right?"

She nodded.

"Fine. Jess, you're a beautiful woman but definitely weird."

"More than likely." Her cell phone rang. "Excuse me." She answered the call from Jordan, her best friend's husband.

"Jess, it's Jordan. Randi and I are on our way."

"Great, thanks." Closing her phone, Jess passed on the information. Jordan worked for her stepmom. He was the newest resident of Squabbin Bay. Of course in a couple months he would lose the title because Randi, Jess's best friend since she was five, would be having a baby, making him or her the newest member of the small seacoast community.

Krispin pushed his chair out from under the table. "I'm fine. I don't need a babysitter. It's not necessary."

"Actually"—she placed her hands on her hips—"I think it is. You didn't eat, and I suspect you haven't taken your medication. Someone needs to look after you, and I can't. Sorry." There was a peculiar attraction to the man, but she couldn't run with such thoughts, and she certainly couldn't enter into a relationship with someone who didn't believe the same as she did. No, it was best if she and Krispin never saw one another again. "If you have any questions, you can contact our attorney."

"Thank you."

"I'm sorry."

"You've already said that."

I know, but I still feel guilty. "Good night, Mr. Black. I'll be praying for you."

He opened his mouth to say something, then closed it.

Jess slipped out of the cottage before she said another word or gave thought to her foolish feelings. *It must be the guilt I'm feeling, Lord.*

two

Krispin drummed his steering wheel, feeling like a fool, waiting in the Squabbin Bay Community Church parking lot on Sunday afternoon. How he'd ever committed himself to having dinner with Randi and Jordan, he'd never understand. Of course they'd hoped he would come to church and join them before they went to the Dockside Grill. He inhaled the lightly seasoned salt air and calmed himself. Finally, people slowly streamed out of the church, laughing and talking with one another. His memories as a child were of hustling into the car to get home for dinner. And the memories of family fights to and from church still turned his stomach in knots.

Person after person, family after family came out, actually happy to be with one another. Jess came out with her parents, he could only assume. And tagging behind them were Randi and Jordan. All five were in a lively discussion. Jess's eyes met his, and she sobered, then nodded her head in his direction. Randi waved.

Krispin gave a weak wave in return.

The man he assumed to be Jess Kearns's father came up to his car. Krispin braced himself for the oncoming wrath. The prospect of a lawsuit and losing his boat and income probably had him in an uproar. Not that Krispin was going to sue. He'd pretty much decided not to after listening to Randi and Jordan talk about the community. He'd learned the red Mercedes belonged to Jess's stepmother.

"Hello, Mr. Black." Mr. Kearns extended his hand. "I'm Wayne Kearns. Jess is my daughter."

Krispin gave a firm handshake but didn't say a word.

"Randi and Jordan just told us they invited you to dinner

with them. You're welcome to come with us, as well."

Krispin's mouth went dry. "Ah, thanks, but no." *Why are these people being so nice?*

"No problem—thought I'd ask."

Wayne Kearns's strides were long and confident as he stepped back to the small group of people. The man was large enough to squash someone if he wanted to, Krispin mused, as Randi and Jordan parted from their friends and headed toward him. Jordan opened the passenger door and sat down. "I'll show you the way. Randi's going to drive our car."

"I could follow."

"Nah, she told me Jess wanted some private time with her. They grew up together. They're pretty close.

"I don't think you told me. . . ." Jordan chattered on. "What do you do for a living?"

They enjoyed some light conversation on the way to the restaurant, Krispin's hands nearly sliding off his steering wheel. *Why am I so nervous?*

"We're here." Jordan pointed to a gray, weathered, shingled building that sat on the edge of the rocky cliff overlooking the harbor.

The same harbor where he'd almost drowned. His hands remained firmly gripped on the steering wheel as if holding on to life. . .his life. It could end so suddenly. Krispin shook off his musings. *No need to dwell on such thoughts.*

"So—what do you recommend?" Krispin closed the door of the car and hoped he sounded calmer than he felt. He watched Randi drive up with Jess. His stomach flipped. He felt trapped. Did he see her as the grim reaper?

"Lobster bisque is one of my favorites." Jordan chuckled.

There had to be some inside joke going on that he didn't understand. Randi joined them, but Jess, he noticed, walked away from the restaurant.

"I'm not partial to lobster."

Jordan sobered. "No problem. They have several different

dishes to choose from."

Randi came up beside them; Jordan looped his arm around his wife's shoulders. It would be nice to find someone who made his life complete. An image of Jess Kearns floated through his mind. He turned his gaze back to the harbor. Nope, that woman was dangerous, in more ways than one.

"Shall we?" Randi motioned for them to go into the restaurant.

Krispin found the Dockside Grill charming, fitting for the area. He noticed Jess's parents eating quietly in a back corner, their gazes locked on one another. *Aren't they curious about me? Doesn't it bother them that I'm going to sue? Or threatened to sue,* he amended.

"Krispin," Randi spoke, "did Jordan tell you this is where he and I met?"

"No, he left out that tidbit. Why don't you tell me?"

Randi elaborated on how the two of them met over a spilled bowl of lobster bisque. Now Krispin knew the inside joke and chuckled along with his hosts.

After lunch they went to the studio where Randi showed off Jordan's work. He was a good photographer, Krispin had to admit. They could use someone like him in his office.

"Have you ever thought of working closer to civilization?" Krispin asked.

"Started in the city. . . it's been more profitable here. The money was fair, but the other benefits far outweigh life in the city. At least for me." Jordan winked at his wife. "Of course I was straight out of college and full of myself back then, but I like it here. Plus, Randi and I want to raise our children in Squabbin Bay."

Krispin had learned yesterday that Randi was expecting their first child which, from her expanding waistline, now seemed obvious. "Would you be interested in some freelance?"

"Possibly. You'd have to talk with Dena. She arranges my schedule."

"Is she an agent?"

Jordan nodded. "Of sorts. She's actually a far better photographer than myself. But she's semi-retired and concentrating on her marriage and family over career these days. Perhaps you've seen some of her work. Her name is Dena Russell."

"Doesn't ring a bell." But apart from Ansel Adams, Krispin knew no other photographer's name.

"Too bad. Here, let me show you." And for the next thirty minutes Krispin was treated to some of Dena's photographs.

Krispin slipped his hands into his pockets and placated his host—until he spotted a picture so terrifying he gasped out loud.

2a.

Jess picked up another pebble and tossed it onto the water. It skipped four times before it sank. In her younger years, she and her father had played for hours, skipping stones and talking. She rocked gently back on her heels, remembering. Yesterday after their Sunday lunch, Jess, Randi, and her stepmother had talked about Jess's frustration with wanting to be a good witness to Krispin. After her experience with Trevor, her college boyfriend, she was leery about getting involved with any man, and certainly didn't want a relationship with one who didn't believe in God.

She replayed the accident over and over in her mind, trying to figure out where he'd come from and why she hadn't seen him cross her path.

"Jess?" Krispin Black's smooth baritone voice played down her spine.

She turned toward the voice as her back stiffened, forcing herself to remain neutral to any emotions she might have. "Mr. Black."

"You didn't come to lunch yesterday."

How'd he know I was out here? "Are you tracking me down?"

"No. Well, yes, I suppose I am. I'm going to be staying an additional week and was wondering if you'd be interested in going out to dinner with me?"

Jess snickered. "You're suing me *and* you want me to go out to dinner? Is this for a tactical advantage at the trial?"

"There won't be a trial. Most lawsuits are handled out of court."

"I don't get it." Jess placed her hands on her hips. "We're more than willing to compensate for your losses, so why sue?"

Krispin shrugged and looked down at his feet. Slowly he lifted his head and locked his gaze with hers. A smile rose on his lips. "Tell ya what. If you go out with me, I won't sue your dad for his entire company."

"Blackmail?"

"Now, did I say anything about blackmail? I'm merely suggesting that if you'll give me the pleasure of your company, I'll reduce the scope of the lawsuit."

"Mr. Black, I'm sorry to say I don't like you. Why would you even care to go out with me?"

He reached out for her, then held back. Or she stepped back. Jess wasn't exactly sure.

"You nearly killed me, Ms. Kearns. The very least you could do—"

"I also saved your life," she interrupted. "I am not duty bound to go out with you. There's no attraction," she mumbled.

He squinted.

"What I mean to say is that while you might be a handsome enough man, your personality is limited. And there is the issue of my Christian faith, which you don't share. I will not date a man who does not believe as I do. Once was enough," she confessed. *Why'd I say that?* she chided herself.

"I'm really a decent person, once you get to know me."

"I suppose that's in the eye of the beholder." Jess stepped away from the water's edge. She didn't like being rude to anyone, but Mr. Krispin Black grated her nerves, in positive and negative ways.

"Touché." He bowed and turned back toward the parking

lot. Halfway to his car, he turned around again. "I won't sue your father."

"Thank you." Tears threatened to fall. For the past three days, she could think of little else except how she had not only ruined her father's business but nearly killed a man, as well.

"I really didn't see you," she choked. "I'm so sorry. I am glad I was able to save you."

He nodded. "Thanks. I shouldn't have been so hard on you. Life's been a. . ." A word Jess would have preferred not to hear escaped his lips.

"Sorry," he apologized. "I've done well in business. The language goes with the territory."

And made you hard as nails. "I'll pray you find more joy in your life, Mr. Black," she said softly.

He plopped down on the beach right where he'd been standing. "I don't get it. Why? I've been miserable to you, to your family. Why do you care?"

Admittedly she had found it hard to care a few moments ago. But now, seeing a more humbled image of the man, her heart was drawn to him. She took a tentative step forward, then stopped. "Because if not for God's grace, I'd be the same as you."

"You?" He snickered. "You have no idea what the corporate world is like."

Jess shook her head. He had her compassion for only a moment. "Mr. Black, do you realize how big your ego is? You make judgments about people without knowing them. You're automatically assuming I've never been in the corporate world, which is a wrong assumption. I was once as driven as you are. Thankfully, it didn't last long. Don't get me wrong, Christians and Christian CEOs have a place in business, but it is a hard line to walk. I was drawn to success first, the Lord second, and possibly even lower, before. . .well, never mind."

"Jessica, I'm sorry."

She nodded rather than say something she would regret. "Have your lawyer contact me when you're ready to file." Jess marched to her car, leaving the man full of himself and his shoes and britches full of sand.

"God, only You can do something with that man. I can't."

❧

Krispin felt as useless as the piece of driftwood lying on the beach in front of him. He'd once had a life. But recently he'd been drifting on the sea, tossed and turned and aged by the world. Had he really turned into a man with such an inflated ego that he prejudged people, and poorly at that?

He grabbed a fistful of sand and let it stream through his fingers, repeating the mindless process several times. Was there really a God who held people? Who held the world, the universe, in the palm of His hand? Randi and Jordan thought so. So did Jess. It was obvious that her family did not respond to his threat the same way a normal person would. *At least not a normal person in my world*, he amended. They'd be looked at as wimps. But Wayne Kearns was no wimp.

Brushing off the sand from his hands, he scanned the horizon. The sea was a royal blue spotted with outcroppings of small green and rock islands. He couldn't sue Jess. As much as Gary, his senior partner, and everyone else would expect him to, he just couldn't. He owed her his life, even if she was the one who had nearly killed him. If she hadn't saved him, he'd be dead now. Krispin paused on that thought. *And what would death be like for me, if there is a God?*

A shiver of fear slid down his spine. He looked toward heaven and cried out, "Are You really up there?"

Not hearing an answer, he paused and listened for a moment longer. Still nothing, except the gentle roll of the surf hitting the shore. He left the beach unsure of life in a way he'd never experienced before. He'd come to Squabbin Bay to find answers. Instead he found more confusion, more pain, more honesty. Was he really a self-centered egomaniac? Not that Jess had said it in quite those terms, but he certainly understood what she'd implied.

three

Jess gasped, tightened her grip on the shopping cart, and pulled it around the corner. Meeting Krispin Black at the beach yesterday had been bad enough, but to see him in the aisle of the grocery store forced her to retreat. Originally she had planned on doing her shopping on Friday, but running over Krispin Black's kayak had unraveled her. With the lawsuit against her looming, she had spent a sleepless night. While it was true she didn't have much, she had managed to purchase a home nearly a year ago. It took four months to work out the paperwork, so technically she'd only owned the house for eight months. There wasn't much equity, but she'd be starting from scratch if Mr. Black did sue her.

"Hello, Ms. Kearns," Krispin said with a smug smile.

"Hello." Jess pushed her cart farther down the aisle. She didn't need anything in this one, having already been down it. She reached for another can of black olives anyway.

"I read over your financial information. You said you didn't have much. You own your own home, Ms. Kearns."

"I have a mortgage, which has only had eight payments made against it out of 360. So if you call that owning, yes, I have a house." She paused and put the can back on the shelf. She also had her deposit and closing costs. "Will you be suing for possession of my house?"

"I can't see the advantage of owning your mortgage."

Jess relaxed. She'd given up trying to understand her attraction to him. Instead she felt it best to simply avoid him as much as possible. But in a town as small as Squabbin Bay, she wasn't sure how easy that would be. "How long are you here for?"

"Originally just the weekend. But because of the accident, I've taken the entire week off."

Jess nodded. Being Tuesday, that meant he'd be in town for four to five more days. And if he was kayaking. . . "Mr. Black, I'd be happy to loan you my kayak while you're visiting our area."

"Seriously?"

"Yes."

"Why?" He raised his eyebrows. His neatly trimmed, dark brown hair didn't seem to match the stubble showing on his face.

"Because it's the right thing to do. And you should get back on the water as soon as possible. I don't know what kind of fears you might have after what you've been through, but I can't imagine it will be too easy for you to go back into the water."

He squared his shoulders. "I can handle it."

"I'm sorry, I don't mean to be telling you your business. I just thought you might like to go kayaking while the weather is agreeable. A front's due to come in tomorrow, and well, you won't be able to kayak on the ocean."

"I hadn't heard the weather forecast. Thank you. If you don't mind, I'd like to take you up on that offer."

"No problem. I'll deliver the kayak to your cottage after I'm done shopping." She turned, placed both hands on the cart, and continued down the aisle. If she worked quickly, she could get to his place before he returned. She hoped.

"What about dinner?"

She stopped short. If nothing else, Krispin Black was a determined individual. Jess could easily see how he'd made his mark in the corporate business world. "I believe we had this conversation yesterday."

"Nothing has changed?"

"Nothing has changed."

"Farewell, Ms. Kearns."

Jess simply nodded. *Finally.* Her shoulders slumped. She was done with Krispin Black. Well, done for the moment. The pending lawsuit still loomed on the horizon.

She scurried to the checkout, went home, and loaded her kayak on the roof of her car. It was a beat-up, old Volkswagen Bug from the sixties that her father managed to keep running from spare parts found in the junkyard. Because it was a classic car, she hoped to refurbish it someday. But other things had been more important, like saving for the house, furniture to put in the house, and supporting the lobstermen's co-op. For the past two years, she'd been working hard at establishing the co-op. The profits from last year were marginal. This year, with the continuation of good weather and healthy catches, they expected to make a good profit.

The phone rang as she opened the screen door to the back porch of her house. She wrestled the bags of groceries into one arm and picked up the cordless phone. "Hello."

"Hey, Jess, it's Myron Buefford."

"Hi, Myron, what can I do for you?" Myron had moved up to Maine from Louisiana thirty years ago after a hurricane had wiped out his shrimping business. He figured while Maine was colder, it seldom had hurricanes. Nor'easters were another matter. But he and his family had settled in. His kids had developed a linguistic blend of Southern and Down-Eastern twang. Myron, on the other hand, still spoke as Southern as if he'd just moved up.

"We heard about the accident and pending lawsuit. We're wondering if ya'll would come to a meeting of the co-op tonight with your attorney. We want to make sure Mr. Black can't own the co-op."

Jess stood rigid for a moment. *Could Krispin Black end up as a member of the co-op? Dear Lord, please say it isn't so.* Then the thought hit her. Incorporation was one of the points her stepmother had made when they were establishing it. "Myron, I think the co-op is covered with the way we set up the Articles of Incorporation, but I'll willingly meet with all of you. And if my lawyer can't be there, I'll ask his take on all of this."

"Thanks, Jess. We all know it was an accident, and the man has to be out of his mind to want to sue. I'm sorry for your troubles, and no one wants y'all out of the co-op." He paused. Jess could see Myron, in her mind's eye, brushing the few strands on top of his head to the back—a gesture he'd been making since she was a little girl and he had a full head of hair. "But we've all worked real hard to establish it."

"Myron, I'll be there. Trust me, I've worked too hard to let this co-op fall into the hands of someone else. I believe we took care of this when we incorporated, but let's be sure."

"You're not upset?"

Jess could hear Myron's wife, Shelia, mumbling something in the background. "Myron, I really understand. I'll do whatever I can to protect the co-op."

"Thanks, Jess. I knew you'd understand."

More than he realized. She'd met with Krispin Black several times now and knew he would be relentless in his pursuit of anything he put his mind to. Unfortunately he didn't put his mind on God. Jess shook her head and ended her conversation with Myron. After she'd put away her groceries, she drove the kayak over to Krispin Black's house. His car was in the drive. Her heart sank. If only he were still at the store.

The back door to his rental cottage squeaked open. "Thanks for bringing the kayak by. Are you certain about the loan, Ms. Kearns?"

"Yes."

"Fine-looking kayak. I don't recognize the brand." His gaze traveled the breadth and length of the long, slim, one-man kayak.

"Dad and I built this about ten years ago."

"Nice." He pulled his gaze from the boat back to her. His royal blue eyes sparkled. "You built this?"

"Yes, with my father. We used to go kayaking every year until I went to college. Unfortunately, I haven't used it enough lately."

"What a shame. It's a fine-looking vessel." He knelt down and passed his hand over the top of the hull. The boat was a wooden-strip kayak with a fiberglass hull. "I don't get to go as often as I used to, either."

"Price of growing up, I guess."

"Or our obsessions. Mine's work. What's yours?" He stood and faced her again.

Jess suppressed the desire to get to know Krispin. *Or did the Lord put him in my life for me to witness to him?*

"What?" She shook her head in confusion. "Look, Mr. Black, I'm uncomfortable speaking with you. One minute you're talking a lawsuit, the next you're asking me to go out with you. Forgive me, but I need to go. I hope you enjoy the kayak. Just leave it here when you go back home, and I'll pick it up." Jess scurried back to her car.

"So, your charity only goes out with regard to your possessions?"

She stopped and turned toward him. How dare he accuse her of not showing the Lord's love to him! She placed her hands on her hips, opened her mouth slightly to rebuff him, then closed it. Why should she get into an argument? "Enjoy your stay in Squabbin Bay, Mr. Black."

Jess slipped behind the wheel. Her hands and body were trembling. It wasn't fear, exactly. The shakes seemed more to do with her controlling her anger. *How dare he presume to judge my faith!*

⟡

Krispin had done it again. Whenever Jessica Kearns came near him, he put up more defenses than the US Army fighting terrorists. *Why?* He honestly didn't have a problem with her and her religion. It just wasn't something he cared about one way or the other. And apart from the cost of a replacement kayak and his medical bills, he didn't need remuneration for the accident. But he continued to fluster Jess with the impending lawsuit. *Why?* Truth was, he would have sued her for every cent he could a year ago. Krispin let out a deep sigh. A year ago. That's when all his dissatisfaction with life began. And whatever he'd thrown at Jessica Kearns, she didn't retaliate. She simply went the extra mile and provided all the information he needed. She offered her home. . .what was she thinking?

He watched the old Volkswagen Bug sputter down the road. The answers he was looking for weren't in Maine; they were back home at work, at his studio apartment, where his life had taken the wrong path. Yes, he needed to return home. Then he could put everything back into its proper perspective.

Inside the cottage he packed his bag, then left an envelope with a healthy tip for the maid service and a note that Jessica Kearns would be back to pick up her kayak in a few days. He drove through the heart of Squabbin Bay. People were chatting with one another. Lobstermen were working on the docks. Wayne Kearns waved as Krispin drove past. Krispin pulled over into a graveled parking spot.

Wayne Kearns left his dock and walked over toward the car. "What can I do for you, Mr. Black?"

Krispin stared down his opposition. "Tell Jess I am only asking for damages and that I'm leaving town, so she can pick up her kayak."

"All right. But didn't she just take it over?"

"Yes. Uh, something came up. I'm heading home earlier than expected."

Wayne Kearns nodded. "Tell me something, Mr. Black. Why did you pick Squabbin Bay for your vacation?"

"I've been under a lot of stress at work and wanted a nice, quiet place to reevaluate my position with the company." Krispin rubbed his hands on the steering wheel.

"I guess the accident changed all that."

Krispin nodded.

"I'll pray you'll make the right decision, Mr. Black."

"A rugged outdoorsman like yourself takes stock in that God stuff?"

Wayne Kearns's smile brightened. "Yes, I do. Wanna talk about it?"

"Not really. I mean no offense. Religion never seemed to matter before. Life is life. You work hard, do your job, be nice to folks, and eventually die one day."

"I suppose that's how your life is. Mine, well, I don't think I would have done so well if I hadn't found the Lord. Jess was nearly two, I was nineteen, a single father, and my life was controlling me. I worked to provide for Jess. I spent every free moment I had with her. I loved her so much, yet something was missing. At first I thought it was that I didn't have a wife. But the answer wasn't in finding more women and a mother for my daughter. The answer came to me when I didn't know what else to do, when I finally gave up trying to do my best and constantly falling short. Truthfully, if I hadn't found God and surrendered to Him, I wouldn't have made it as a single father."

"Where was Jess's mother?"

"She was sixteen when she got pregnant. She agreed to let me keep the baby and raise her. Terry finished school, went on to college, and eventually made a new life for herself. She wasn't ready to be a mother. Not that I was ready to be a father, but I had the advantage of having a mother who would watch Jess while I was working. If it hadn't been for my parents, I wouldn't have made it financially or emotionally. Jesus gave me a peace, a confidence, the strength to go on. And I'm probably sounding like I'm preaching here a bit, but the Bible is a good handbook on how to really enjoy life. After all, God is the creator of life."

Krispin wagged his head. "If you believe all that stuff,

I suppose. It just seems archaic to me."

"You know, you're right. You can't get much more archaic than with God."

"I can see where Jess gets it from."

Wayne narrowed his gaze and leaned a little closer. "I raised her in the church, but she had to find her own way to let God in and give Him the chance to rule over her life. God doesn't have grandchildren, only children, meaning we all have to accept Him as our Father. There isn't a grandfather clause in Christianity."

Krispin raised his right eyebrow. Hadn't his parents always told him he was a Christian, that they had baptized him as a baby? That he had his fire insurance if there was a hell? "So, you don't believe everyone is going to heaven? *If* there is a heaven," he amended.

"Nope. It's a choice, Mr. Black."

"Jordan said something similar the other night when they watched over me because of the concussion."

"Not surprised. He has a pretty solid faith."

"Is everyone in Squabbin Bay like you guys?"

Wayne chuckled. "No. But we have a good-sized church, and we're a fairly strong-willed people when it comes to our faith and living it out. Actually, we can be strong-willed a lot of the time, even when we shouldn't be."

Krispin shifted in his bucket seat, then slid his hand around the steering wheel again. He didn't want to insult the man, but he had to admit he would make any minister proud. Krispin knew Jordan worked for Wayne's wife as a professional photographer and had a huge respect for both Wayne and Dena. Jordan had said Dena's first husband had been a pastor, just like her son was the pastor of the Squabbin Bay Community Church. So it made sense that she'd remarry someone who had a faith equal to that of her first husband. . . if she respected her religion. He supposed it worked for this blended family. "Hey, I'm happy for you, Mr. Kearns. You raised a fine daughter, even if she is dangerous behind the wheel of a boat."

He saw the muscle in Wayne Kearns's jaw move slightly. "For the record, Jess has been driving that boat since she was four, and she's never had an accident. Unfortunately accidents do happen, Mr. Black. I'm sure, over time, Jess will get over nearly killing you. But I think you should be thanking the Lord that she had her wits about her and jumped in and rescued you, rather than securing the boat first. I think that's what saved your life. And given time, I imagine Jess will get over this and be comfortable behind the wheel once again."

"Forgive me; you're right. Thank Jess again for me. I'd better go."

Wayne tapped the lower part of the window doorframe. "All right, Mr. Black. Travel safely."

"Absolutely." Krispin put the car in reverse. Wayne stepped away from the vehicle. Krispin hesitated for a moment, then pulled out. The sooner he put Squabbin Bay in his rearview mirror the better. As uncomfortable as he'd gotten with his life back home, it didn't compare to what he was feeling now. He'd never been so confused or on edge, even when he'd gone through the investigation from the gaming commission regarding the technology he'd written to protect their online Web sites from intruders. While everyone knew of Internet thieves, few had slipped under the radar like the one who got through one of Krispin's encryption programs. Thankfully it was the first layer of encryption, and they'd only escaped with bogus files. The creative thinking he'd put into his program had earned him a partnership in the company. The intense scrutiny made him question why he was living like this.

He drove down the winding road that led out of Squabbin Bay to Route 1, which he'd take to Ellsworth. There he'd pick up Route 1A to Bangor, then Interstate 95 South toward home.

"Why did I pick Squabbin Bay? No one recommended

it. I simply threw a dart at the map and it landed there," he reminded himself. He'd taken to speaking to himself out loud inside the car. It was a way to sort out what was important, what he needed to remember, and besides, he had no one else to talk with.

four

A month later Jess found the letter from Krispin Black waiting in her mailbox. It included his ambulance bill, his hospital bill, and the receipt for the kayak he'd purchased. When he'd left town, Krispin had told her father that he wouldn't be suing her. But she couldn't believe it was true, not until she opened this letter. The actual bill was less than a thousand dollars. She was only paying the co-payment and the cost of a new kayak. What she didn't expect to see in the letter was "plan two," as Krispin called it.

"Jess, if you're willing to help me build a kayak just like yours, I'm willing to absorb all the costs. Can you help me?" He then listed all his contact information.

Jess dropped the paper. He lived in Manchester, New Hampshire. That was an easy four-and-a-half-hour drive. "No way, I'll pay." She stomped over to the phone and called her father.

"Hello," he answered on the second ring.

"Hi, Daddy."

"Hey, Jess, what's up?"

"Krispin Black's bill came in the mail today. He's asking for less than a thousand."

Her father sighed. "Thank the Lord."

"Yeah." Jess paused and curled the cord around her finger. "Daddy, he gave me an alternative to paying the money."

"What's that?" His voice sounded tight.

"He asked me to help him build a kayak like mine."

Her father snickered. "He doesn't quit, does he?"

"No." She'd been open with her parents about Krispin's insistence on going out to dinner. "He lives in Manchester,

New Hampshire. I can't be spending nine hours on the road—"

"There is that. But I think it would be better to simply keep your distance from the man."

"I agree. Besides, the cost is nothing compared to what it could have been."

"True. I'll have Dena write a check in the morning, and you can put it in your account and pay him off."

"No, Daddy. I appreciate it. But I have to pay for this myself. It will be tight, but I can do it."

"Are you sure?"

"Yes, sir." It had taken her the better part of a year to learn how to control her spending and her finances, but she'd done it. Of course using her father's credit card to buy her boyfriend expensive gifts right after graduation from college taught her some heavy-duty lessons, as well. But thankfully she had learned quickly and didn't have any debt, except for her mortgage.

"All right. Thanks for calling, and I'm glad Mr. Black was a man of his word."

A smile curled on the edges of her lips. Yes, Krispin Black had done exactly as he'd said he would. He'd even charged her less than what he could have. "Talk with you later, Dad."

She pushed the Off button on her phone and walked back over to the letter. She opened her laptop computer and typed out an e-mail to Krispin Black.

Dear Mr. Black,
I received your letter today. I'll be sending you a check in a few days.

Sincerely,
Jessica Kearns

Jess hesitated before she sent the e-mail. He'd given her his contact information the night of the accident and again in this letter. She hadn't given him her e-mail address. Did she want him to have it? She paused, thinking on the matter. It would make it easy for him to contact her. But what other contact would they have? Once she sent the money, their association would be finished.

Jess hit the SEND button. For better or worse, she sent it. She could always change her e-mail address or simply not read anything he sent in the future. She sat at the computer for a moment longer, scrolling through her in-box. For the most part, her personal e-mail entailed little notes from friends. There was an e-mail from her biological mother.

Hey Jess,

I'm sorry it took so long to get back with you. Yes, I'm looking forward to your visit. The kids are excited to see their big sister. I'm glad you're doing okay after the accident. What a terrible thing to go through. I'm really glad your faith brings you so much comfort.

I have our entire time together planned out. We'll be going. . .

Jess scanned the itinerary her mother had laid out. If nothing else, Terry, her bio-mom, was organized to the hilt, which was where, she supposed, she got her organizational skills. Her father wasn't unorganized, but he wasn't a neat freak. His record keeping consisted of a container here, a folder in the filing cabinet there, and a couple of coffee cans for each of his business receipts. That was how it had been for years, until Jess had taken over that part of the business while she was in high school, and then again once she returned home from college.

Maintaining a relationship with her bio-mom had been very strained during all of Jess's high school and college years. But for the past two years, since her mom got a computer and discovered the Internet, contact was less strained but still not what it could be. It felt good to have some connection with this woman. She recognized a few of her characteristics in Terry.

Truthfully, she and Terry would never have a real mother-daughter relationship. The most Jess hoped for was a friendship, and that seemed to be getting better. The weekend visit with her mother would prove to be the true test of their new relationship.

Dena, her stepmother, was more of a mother than anyone else had ever been. The fact that they had begun their relationship when Jess was finishing college made it awkward at first to think of this woman as her mother. The plus side of all of this was Dena had raised three kids and knew how to have a good relationship with all of her adult children, even her in-law children. Jess could talk with Dena, and with all Jess's heart, she loved and respected her stepmom.

Terry had been sixteen when she got pregnant, and her parents had not been nurturers. They had even moved away from Squabbin Bay right after Terry finished high school. They had never acknowledged Jess's existence. Instead they encouraged Terry to have an abortion. They never wanted their daughter tied down to a child, certainly not one born out of wedlock. Jess honestly didn't hold any resentment toward these people. They just never factored into her life. Her father's parents had been wonderful grandparents whom she loved dearly.

Jess's thoughts drifted back to the screen, and she typed in a reply to her mother. Her in-box contained an e-mail from Krispin Black. Hesitantly she clicked it open.

Dear Jess,
  Thanks. Take your time with the check. I won't be replacing the kayak for a while.

Krispin

Jess relaxed her shoulders. "Thank You, Lord. He didn't

push the idea of my helping him build a kayak."

∾

Krispin pushed himself away from his desk and looked out his office window. The building his company now owned had once been a linen factory. Below was the Merrimack River, the power source that had kept the machines working for many years. He loved that about the old building. His office, like the rest of the others in his company, was a totally contemporary one. High-tech lighting, furniture, computers, and lots of white, black, and stainless steel metal with wooden-framed windows and cream-colored walls. It was a blend of the old and new.

Gary tapped on Krispin's office doorjamb. "Krisp, got a minute?" His voice sounded more subdued than usual. Of course the fact that Krispin had only four more days with the company might have something to do with it.

"Sure." Krispin put the tiny flash drive in his pocket. He'd backed up all of his files to download onto his computer. While he'd given his resignation a few days after returning from Maine, he had agreed to work as a consultant from time to time and to be the technical advisor on some of his more sophisticated encryption programs.

By the time Krispin walked out into the hallway, Gary was striding into his office. Gary was like that, always business, all the time. Gary hadn't so much as flinched when Krispin had handed in his typewritten letter.

"Come in, close the door," Gary said as he settled in behind his glass-topped desk.

Krispin sat down. "What's up?"

Gary closed his eyes and paused. "Krisp, I thought you'd have changed your mind by now. Please, tell me what I need to do for you to stay with the company. Name it, and it's yours."

Krispin leaned back in his chair. "I've lost my edge, Gary. I'm no good to you or the company."

"Hogwash. Look, you can work from home. . .from across the world. I don't care. I don't want to lose you. You saved our bacon too many times. I need that brain of yours working for me."

"Gary, you have my word. I've signed all the contracts. I'll never reveal the codes. You know that."

Gary folded his hands and padded his thumbs together three times. It was one of those habits his partner exhibited under stress. Gary's showed up when he wasn't getting his way. "I know. Besides, I'll sue you for everything you've got and your future earnings if you *ever* break one of our contracts."

Krispin's spine tightened. A flicker of Jessica Kearns displaying the same reaction when he threatened to sue passed before his mind's eye. *Interesting.* "You and I both know that will never be the case; that's why you agreed to buy my portion of the company."

"That's the part that bugs me, Krisp. After all this time, you allowed me to buy you out. You could have held on to your share, maintained your interest in the company. If you did that, I wouldn't have had nightmares every night for the past three weeks. What gives? You and I have been at this for seven years."

"All the more reason to trust me, don't you think?" Krispin shifted in his chair.

Gary narrowed his gaze. "Is this that God junk you've been philosophizing about?"

"No." *Was it?* His mind hadn't been able to settle on anything about anything since leaving Squabbin Bay. "Nah, I was considering this when I left for vacation, Gary, and that was my first vacation in five years. I'm burned out."

Gary raised his hands in surrender. "All right." He lifted a small bundle of papers. "Here's the check and the contracts. Have your lawyer go over them. Legal's gone over them with a fine-toothed comb, but you need an attorney. I won't have it any other way."

"All part of the corporate process. Not a problem." Krispin took the pages from Gary. "Gary, I do appreciate all that you've done for me and my career."

Gary nodded. "Don't make me regret my decisions, Krisp."

"You won't. And I promised to be available for consultations."

"You and I both know that will only last for a short time. The industry changes too fast to be out of the loop for more than six months."

"I understand."

"So on a personal note, where are you going? What are you going to do with yourself?"

Find myself? How sixtyish does that sound? "I've rented a cottage for the summer months in Maine."

"That must have set you back a bundle."

"Not too bad." Squabbin Bay was remote enough that summer rentals were easy to come by. Not that Krispin felt inclined to tell Gary that secret tidbit he'd discovered quite by accident while searching for a place last month.

"Well. . ." Gary held out his hand. Krispin got up and shook it. "I'll see you around."

"Thanks, Gary."

Gary nodded, picked up his phone, and punched in a number. Krispin left the room like so many other times before, unsure of his place in the company. That was just Gary's way. Some of the folks who had come to work for them had quit because they didn't like Gary's personality, or lack thereof. It never bothered Krispin, never until today. Why now?

Because it's directed at you, he reminded himself, and exited Gary's office as swiftly as possible. Twenty steps later he was alone in his office, looking down at the Merrimack River. Krispin leafed through the pages and looked at the six-figure sum on the check. In two years it would have been three times as much. Was it worth it? Was Squabbin Bay the only place he could deal with this God issue?

He'd given up on not believing. God seemed plausible,

but Krispin knew he had to change his life. He wasn't even thirty years old and already feeling like he'd lived a lifetime with little or nothing to show for it. All his accolades meant nothing in the grand scheme of things. If he wanted to, he could have worked, or still could work, on encryption programs from any remote location that had a strong Internet connection. He knew from Randi and Jordan that the only high-speed access to the Internet in Squabbin Bay was provided by a satellite service. He'd been working on computer programming since he was twelve. Mathematics he understood. He had even downloaded the Bible onto his iPod. God stuff. . .well, that didn't make sense.

He glanced at the check again. If frugal, he could live for many years off this check. Or he could invest the money. He didn't need to decide at the moment. His phone rang, jarring him back to the office work that still needed to be done before he left the company.

Five calls later and at least an hour on the computer, everything in his office was purged of his personal information. Once he removed the couple of boxes containing his personal belongings, there would be little evidence that he'd worked here for the past seven years. He looked at the family pictures that used to sit on a small table between two chairs. His parents stood arm in arm with a picture of Haleakala Crater on Maui in the Hawaiian Islands. The crater supported no vegetation, no life, just rock and rubble from the old volcano. He'd thought it odd they would see the photo as picturesque, but then again, he'd given them the trip as an anniversary present.

He picked up the simple wooden frame and brushed the glass with his thumb. He loved his family, but he wasn't close to any of them. They'd been brought up to be totally independent of one another. Conversation at the table that involved getting to know what one or the other had been doing rarely happened. They ate together because that was the rule of the house. But conversation wasn't a part of it. Conversation at a dinner table took on a whole new meaning when he went to college. Everyone talked. People gathered in small groups and talked about everything. The first few months Krispin offered little into the conversations. But slowly, as time passed, he'd speak more and more, to the point where he decided he liked this level of conversation. He discovered that many families used that time to connect with one another. He wondered if Jess experienced that with her family. Somehow, he imagined they probably did. Mr. Kearns didn't seem like the kind of man to keep his personal opinions to himself. The day Krispin left Squabbin Bay, he'd given Krispin a lot to think about.

"Hey, Krispin." Judy Enwright stood at the door. They had dated several years ago. But Judy had wanted more than a casual relationship. He decided from then on he wouldn't date any of the women who worked for the company.

"Hi, Judy. What can I do for you?"

"Just wanted to say good-bye." Judy stepped closer. Her eyes burned with desire. Krispin turned around and picked up one of the boxes as a shield.

She reached out and placed her hand on his arm. "Since you're no longer going to work here, whadaya think about us getting back together again?"

No way. "Judy, I'm flattered, but I'm leaving town, leaving the state. Long-distance relationships never work out."

"What about. . ."

"Judy, thanks, but no thanks."

"Well, I never!" Judy huffed.

Krispin tried to soften the blow. "Judy, you and I weren't a good match. I'm sorry. You're better off trying to find the right man than just any man. I'm sorry I used you."

Judy's eyes watered.

Krispin put down the box and cradled her in his arms. "I'm so sorry. It was a mistake."

Judy sniffed. "I know. But. . ."

"Shh, don't you worry any more about this. I'll be praying for you to find someone." At that moment Krispin knew he really would be praying for her and for all the other women he'd used in his past. He felt like a cad, totally unworthy of anyone's love. He had abused love, used love to get what he wanted. He had never really loved anyone. "I was horrible to use you that way. I'm very sorry."

"You pray? I thought you didn't have any use for God."

"I don't. I mean, I didn't." Krispin released Judy and picked up the box. "Judy, I don't know much about God, but I'm trying to learn."

"Is this why you're leaving? To go find God like a monk or something?"

Krispin let out a nervous chuckle. "You know, Judy, I hadn't thought about it like that before, but I guess you're right. I'm going to live like a monk."

"Man, that's just crazy."

"More than likely, but I'm not good enough for anyone right now. I can't function in business, and my personal life is zilch. I don't know who or what I believe in at this point in time. Trust me, you're better off not knowing me."

Judy laughed. "You weren't that great to begin with."

"Gee, thanks."

Judy laughed again. "See ya around, Krispin. I can't picture you living like a monk. Good luck."

Krispin knew he was getting into this God stuff probably a little too deeply. Then again, maybe not. Hopefully he'd find the answers he was looking for. He hadn't found them in success, in women, in adventures—everything he'd experienced in life to this point had left him dry and unfulfilled. *Why?*

five

Jess clicked the power switch to the winch, which pulled the pot out of the water and up to the side of the boat. The power winch and pulley were something she'd purchased to make her life a little easier. Her father had hauled the pots up by hand for years, but even he admitted to liking the new system.

She hoisted the metal cage on board, took out the four lobsters, and placed in a new bait bag. The boat rolled with the waves. Her sea legs held, and all was right in the world. Krispin Black was no longer a threat, and the monthly meeting of the co-op last night had breathed a collective sigh of relief. No one was more grateful than Jess.

The memory of Krispin, pale faced, lying on the dock, floated back into her mind. It had been six weeks since the chilling event, and still his image was as real as when it actually happened. Flashbacks came more than once a day. She blinked away the image and praised the Lord that Krispin Black was still alive. "Lord, thank You again for helping me spare Krispin's life. Be with him right now, Lord. Make him aware of You and Your love and grace for him." She had started praying for Krispin that way right after he left town.

She was grateful to see no more messages from Krispin Black in the weeks since he'd replied to her e-mail. The check had been mailed to him yesterday morning, a fact that the entire co-op had been pleased to hear. All thought Mr. Black to be a fair and honorable man. Of course they didn't know of his rude suggestions. Dena and her father knew, but no one else. Jess hadn't even told Randi, though she rarely saw her old friend anymore. Marriage and expecting a baby had a way of changing a person's desire to hang out with single friends. Or maybe it didn't change the desire but kept a young woman busy with other, more important things. She and Randi still talked, just not as often.

"I need a new best friend." Jess plopped the lobster pot back into the Atlantic. Krispin's image popped back into her mind. Jess laughed out loud. "No way."

She finished with the last pot as the sun stood over the horizon and started to warm everything with its golden rays.

"Jess, come back," the radio crackled.

Jess picked up the old bulky gray microphone. "Hey, Dad. Over."

"Just thought I'd warn you before you came in this morning. Word has it Krispin Black is back in town. Rented the same cottage for the summer. Over."

Great. "Thanks. Over."

"Jess, are you going to be okay with this? Over."

"I'll be fine, Dad. Thanks for letting me know. Over."

"Over and out."

Jess returned the mike to the hook. If she could go days and weeks without speaking with her best friend, then it ought to be as easy as sliding on ice to avoid Krispin Black. And that's what she intended to do.

⁂

Two weeks later, Jess caught her first glimpse of Krispin Black in the grocery store.

"Hello," he said as he walked past her, pushing his cart farther down the aisle.

"Hi," she replied. A bit stunned that he didn't say anything else, she felt tempted to turn her cart around and follow him. But she remembered their last conversation in this very store. Jess finished her shopping and headed out to the car.

As she placed the last bag into the trunk and pulled down the hood of her VW Bug, she saw him nearby, getting into an old, completely restored Mustang. *Daddy's dream car*, she mused. "My dad would be so jealous if he saw your car."

Krispin chuckled. "I picked it up when I was fourteen from an older lady who had saved it for her son when he went off to fight in the Vietnam War. I mowed her lawn and took care of her hedges for two years to pay for the car."

"Impressive. You didn't strike me as the mechanical type."

"I'm not." He leaned against the side of his car and folded his arms across his chest. "But I wanted that car. Rot and decay had taken their toll after twenty years, but I've enjoyed refurbishing it."

"Why are you here?" she blurted out, and slapped a hand over her mouth.

"It's all right, Jess. I understand your reluctance to have me in the area. I want to apologize for my behavior before. It was crude, rude, and socially unacceptable. I came here to reevaluate things."

But why here? she wanted to ask, deciding against it. There was no sense getting to know this man further. "See you around."

Krispin nodded and immediately turned away from her. *Is he trying to stay away from me as much as I'm trying to avoid him?*

❧

Krispin squeezed the steering wheel, trying to rein in his frustrations. He'd been debating moving to Squabbin Bay ever since deciding to try and live his life like a monk. He knew Jess would be a temptation to break the commitment. She was more beautiful than he remembered. On the other hand, given the opportunity, they could become friends, he was certain of that. But he wasn't ready to handle friends. He wasn't ready to handle much of anything yet.

Ten days earlier he'd managed to get up the nerve to confront his questions of faith, the Bible, and religion in general and had met with Pastor Russell, the pastor of the same church where he had met Jordan and Randi the Sunday after the accident. Not knowing where else to go, he settled on that church because he trusted the few people he'd met from there. During that meeting Pastor Russell had led Krispin in a prayer of commitment to God. His body trembled at the awesome leap of faith he was making, yet a peace washed over him unlike any he'd experienced before.

But Krispin had put off going to church in order to avoid seeing Jess. He prayed for her daily. He knew she wouldn't appreciate his presence in town. Not that he would blame her. His suggestive tones and comments had been completely out of line. But it felt good to apologize to her.

He turned the key, and the engine roared to life. Earlier that morning, he'd signed a lease to rent one of the old warehouses. He didn't have a place to build a kayak at his cottage and found the old fishing warehouse to be perfect for his needs. The closer it came to building the boat, the more nervous he felt about being able to do it. He'd never done anything like it before. Restoring the car had been easy. He'd simply purchased the refurbished parts and put them in. If he couldn't do it, he had hired someone who could.

This project he planned to do by himself with a little help from an online forum for kayak builders. He'd read and reread all about building the small boats. He now owned enough tools to make any carpenter proud. Learning how to use the tools would take a lot more practice. Purchasing a bunch of wood to get a feel for cutting and gluing seemed the practical way to go. With any luck he'd be able to build something that would float. In truth, he'd love to have someone show him how to use the various tools. Thankfully, detailed videos and instruction manuals could be found on the Internet, not to mention the home makeover shows on television.

Krispin drove to the cottage he had rented for the summer. He had sublet his condo in Manchester for the next six months. If all went well in Squabbin Bay, he'd stay the full time. If life in this secluded area didn't work out, he'd relocate someplace else for a while. His desire was to stay put until he understood what having God in his life meant. He understood he was going to heaven, but living the Christian life day to day would prove difficult, he imagined. So many of his worldviews were turning upside down. Some blended well with scripture, like being kind to people, not murdering anyone, and other basic moral truths. But the reality that his morals weren't the same as God's standard was hitting him hard. He felt an even greater responsibility to all the women he'd known. And truthfully, he knew he wasn't worthy of someone like Jessica Kearns. From everything he'd seen and heard around town, she was a good, clean, and wholesome person. Unlike himself.

When he arrived at the cottage, he found the red light of his answering machine flashing. He pushed the button. "Hi, Krispin, it's Pastor Russell. I'm having a barbecue at my house tonight. If you'd like to come, you're more than welcome. Call me."

Krispin froze. Should he go to such an event? He felt too unworthy to be around the pastor and his family. Krispin picked up the phone and dialed the pastor's number.

"Hello," Pastor Russell answered on the first ring.

"Pastor Russell, Krispin here. Thanks for the offer, but I'm busy tonight."

"Oh, all right. Maybe next time."

"Yeah, maybe," Krispin mumbled.

"Krispin? Is everything all right?"

"Yeah, I'm fine. I've been reading the Bible like you suggested. I'm still having trouble understanding some of it, but I'm seeing more and more of my life as being unfit for God."

"Ah, well, just remember, your sins were forgiven when you asked Jesus into your heart. Everything from your past has been wiped clean. In fact the Bible tells us God throws our sins into the depths of the sea. In other words He forgives and forgets."

"How? I remember them."

"Because He, being God, is able to forgive and forget. We, being human, have a hard time doing that. Even harder is forgiving ourselves for the things we've done." Pastor Russell paused. "Krispin, would you like to talk some more about this? I've got an hour I can spare before family arrives."

"Thanks, but I'll be fine. I'm sorry to impose on your time."

"Like I said before, you're not an imposition. If you change your mind, you're still welcome to come for dinner."

"Thanks. I appreciate the offer."

"You're welcome. Forgive yourself, Krispin. You're a new creature in Christ. Your slate has been wiped clean."

Krispin couldn't quite put his head around that thought. But it made sense on some level. A hard drive can be wiped clean, but what was on it was still there until it was written over many, many times. Just how clean was God's hard drive? "Thanks, I'll keep that in mind."

They said their good-byes, and Krispin went to work putting his groceries away, including the two frozen dinners he had purchased. Eating out, even ordering takeout, was getting boring in Squabbin Bay. Lobster wasn't his favorite food. He could purchase a steak rather than go to the Dockside Grill. Cooking for one had never been one of his favorite things to do. Girlfriends and dates had come in handy with regard to dinners. Picking up fast food for lunch, ordering with the others in the office, all seemed to work just fine and provided an eclectic menu. Adjusting his eating habits was just one of the many obstacles involved in moving to a place so far away that it boasted only one traffic light—a blinking one at that—and one grocery store. Secluded places like this were good for vacations for someone who hadn't grown up here—but not regular life.

On the other hand, those were the very reasons he'd come to such an out-of-the-way place to reexamine his life and priorities. He sighed. Living here would definitely be an adjustment.

Jess watched Jason set the phone in the cradle. "You invited Krispin Black to dinner?"

"Yes, is that a problem?"

How do I answer that? "Well, kinda."

"Jess, I know he threatened a lawsuit."

Jess waved it off. "That isn't the problem."

"Then what is?"

"Nothing. Never mind. Is he coming?"

"No, I don't believe so."

"Okay, whatever." Jess scurried off. *How do you tell your pastor, who's also your stepbrother, your fears of being attracted to such an ungodly man? You don't,* she reminded herself, and went back to the kitchen to help her stepbrother's wife. "Hey, Marie, what can I do to help?"

"Grab the potatoes off the stove and drain them, please."

"Sure." Jess took the hot pot over to the sink and poured the contents into the colander. "What else?"

"How are your potato salad skills?"

"I've gotten much better since I learned Dena's recipe."

"Great, make that. The family loves it."

Jess chuckled. "Where's the bowl?"

"Third cabinet on your right. Everything else is in the fridge."

"Got it." Jess went to work. She wanted to ask Marie why Jason would be inviting Krispin Black to the family picnic. Of course the man needed salvation, and with Jason's job, it probably went hand in hand, him wanting to reach out to a lost soul. *But still. . .why now? Why here?* She was filled with so many questions. She wasn't afraid of Krispin. She was afraid of her own reactions to him.

"Hi, Marie. Hi, Jess." Dena walked into the room, carrying a pan of double-chocolate brownies and a two-gallon cooler of grape lemonade, and set them on the table.

"Hi, Mom," Marie and Jess said in unison.

"So what can I do, Marie?" Dena went straight to the sink and washed her hands.

"Marinate the steaks."

"No problem."

"I'm so—o—o glad you decided on beef tonight," Jess purred. "I've seen too much seafood lately."

Dena chuckled. "Your father can still lobster, Jess. You don't have to do it every morning."

"Yeah, I know, but I don't have too much to do with the co-op right now. Come fall, Dad's going to have to go out pretty near every morning."

"You've spoiled him. He probably won't want to lobster."

Dad came in carrying a huge watermelon and kissed all three women on the cheek. "Hey now, I resent that remark."

Jason followed him in. "Amber and David should be here in a couple minutes."

"Chad and Brianne will be here after she finishes feeding the baby," Dena offered.

Dena's cheerful smile set Jess thinking back on all the planning and how much it meant to Dena to have the entire family together. Oddly enough, Jess felt fully a part of this family. Dena had a way of doing that. Unlike her own mother, Terry. Their visit last week had been strained on several occasions. Jess felt like Terry was trying too hard. Terry's other children and husband weren't all that thrilled with Jess's visit. And despite their obvious discomfort with her visiting, she knew she'd go to her bio-mom's house for a visit again. But she didn't have the same sense of belonging and being a real member of the family like she did here.

"Hello, anyone in here?"

Jess's eyebrows lifted. "Grandpa?"

She turned toward the doorway where her grandfather stood, nodding and grinning warmly. Grandpa and Grandma Kearns hadn't come back to Squabbin Bay since the lobster poaching charges against him had been dropped.

Jess left the potato salad and ran to her grandparents. "Grandma, Grandpa." She hugged them hard. Tears edged her eyes. "It's so good to see you."

"And you, sweet one." Grandma Kearns smiled.

"I love you, princess. I'm sorry." Grandpa hugged her. He'd been guilty of gambling in Florida and had lost just about everything he owned. Jess's father had to bail him out financially, leaving her dad with no money going into his marriage with Dena. At first Grandpa had been bitter and angry. Then as time passed and he got the help he needed, he accepted he was addicted to gambling and had ruined his retirement, life, and reputation. If the community of Squabbin Bay hadn't loved him so much before he had his problems, he would have served a lot of time in prison. In the end, he was doing well. And Grandma Kearns now handled the finances.

"Grandpa, I forgave you a long time ago. You know that."

"I know. I just wanted to say it in person."

Her father placed his hands on her shoulders. "Hey, Mom, Dad. It's good to see you."

"Good to see you too, son. How's that pretty wife of yours?" Grandpa Kearns winked.

"She's just fine. How was your trip, Mom?"

"Fine. I'm a little stiff, but your father stopped just before we got here so we could walk around a bit and stretch our legs and joints." Jess's father gave his mother a kiss on the cheek.

Jess thought back on all the hurt that her father had gone through when he discovered his own father had been the cause of everyone's misfortune that summer. *Forgiveness is a wonderful gift, Lord. Thanks.*

She slipped away from her father and grandparents and made her way toward the kitchen. The house buzzed with people as everyone arrived. Six children, eleven adults, two dogs, one cat, and a pet frog running about made up the entire gathering. Jess loved her family. And they loved her. What more could she want?

A man who loves me, her heart cried out to God. *Not just any man, the right man,* she amended. Trevor had proved to be such a huge disappointment in the boyfriend department that she didn't even want to date anymore.

The doorbell rang. Jason went to answer it. Jess glanced up to see Krispin Black. She swallowed and walked back to the kitchen.

six

Krispin paused. He'd tried to avoid Jess by coming early to explain his actions about not accepting the pastor's invitation, yet there she was. . . *I should have known better.* "Welcome, Krispin. Let me introduce you." Pastor Russell pulled him through the front door while shaking Krispin's hand.

A whirlwind of names swirled around him as he greeted each one. "I'm sorry to intrude, Pastor Russell. But I was wondering if I could borrow you for a moment. I promise it won't take too long."

"Sure. Excuse me, folks." Jason Russell escorted Krispin to his private office in his home. Once inside the small room, Krispin's palms began to sweat. "Pastor, I need to confess something to you."

"Relax, Krispin. Take a seat. What do you feel you need to confess?"

"I turned down your dinner invitation because of Jessica Kearns. You probably know I threatened to sue her."

Pastor Russell nodded.

"Well, it's worse than that. I made a crude comment to her, suggesting a way she could pay me back without using money."

"I see. So you're avoiding church in order to avoid Jess?"

"Yes. I don't want to make her more uncomfortable. I knew it was a problem returning to Squabbin Bay, but I also knew that if I were going to find the answers about God, I'd find them here. Should I leave town?"

"Have you apologized?"

"Yes, but. . ." Krispin rubbed the back of his neck. "It's

not that easy. I'm attracted to her. She's a temptation to my newfound faith. I've been attracted to her from the moment my eyes focused and saw her leaning over me. But I can't have a woman in my life."

"I understand. I'll speak to Jess."

"No, please don't. I mean, I don't want her to think I became a Christian to have her. I can't see how I'd be worthy of any woman's love, but if God sees fit one day, I'd like the woman, even Jess, to be able to see my faith in Christ first. Does that make sense?"

"Yeah, it does. All right, I won't tell Jess. And I'll be mindful to invite you when Jess isn't coming, how is that?"

"Wonderful." Krispin sighed and got up from his chair. "I won't keep you from your family. I just couldn't live with myself, deceiving you."

Pastor Russell extended his hand. "Thanks for filling me in."

Krispin took the proffered hand. "Thanks for not knocking me out for my crude remarks to Jess."

Pastor Russell tightened his hand around Krispin's. "I'm human, Krispin. And I understand you weren't saved, but even by human standards, that was a very rude proposition."

"Yes, sir."

"Remember, she *is* my sister."

"Yes, sir."

"Good. Now, go on home, and I'll handle the family."

"Thank you." Krispin exited the house by way of the front hall, missing the glances from the living room. As he closed the door behind him, he saw Jess with her hands across her chest and a stance that meant she wasn't about to be bullied around. "Hi, Jess."

"What was that about?"

"I needed to apologize to Pastor Russell for turning down his dinner invitation."

"Why?"

Krispin swallowed. He wasn't ready for this conversation. "It's personal, Jess. Can we leave it at that?"

Her eyes widened. "Why are you here, Krispin?"

"I just told you."

"No, I mean here in Squabbin Bay."

"It seemed like the right place to be."

"What about work?"

"I sold my partnership back to the others."

"Why?"

"Jess, forgive me, but these things are my personal matters, not yours."

She opened her mouth, then closed it. "You're right. I'm sorry."

"Jess, I do have one question for you. Would it be a problem for you if I went to church?"

"You?"

Krispin looked down at the ground and scuffed his shoe against the pavement. "Yeah, me. Would you have a problem if I attended here?"

"Ah, no, I guess not. Are you sure?"

Never more sure of anything in my entire life. "Yeah, I'd like to hear Pastor Russell preach."

"I can't stop you from coming to church, Krispin. It's a free country. You can go to whatever church you like."

"Thanks, I promise to stay out of your way. Good-bye, Jess."

"Bye."

Krispin felt her penetrating gaze sear his shoulders as he walked back toward town and to his cottage. All in all, things went very well. He didn't confess to Jess that he was now a believer. He'd rather have her see it in his life.

❧

Jess returned to the family with a million questions. The first and foremost was what was going on with Krispin Black. He seemed almost lost, but not really. He didn't seem as arrogant as he had after she'd nearly killed him. Had she caused the man to lose his drive, convictions? *Dear Lord, say it isn't so.*

"Jess, what's the matter?" Dena came up beside her and wrapped a loving arm around her shoulders.

"Hey, Mom, sorry."

"Is it Krispin Black?"

Jess nodded.

"Did he do anything?" Jess felt Dena stiffen.

"No, nothing like that. He seems different. Less of a man somehow. I'm afraid the accident took away who he was."

"You know the Lord could have used that to get ahold of him."

"I suppose. He's just so unsure of himself. He didn't make one leering comment."

"Well, that's a good sign."

Jess chuckled. "I guess it is. I've just come to expect a certain behavior from him, and when I didn't see it, it bothered me."

"Honey, I'm glad he wasn't rude again. But I still don't think it's wise for you to be alone with him."

"Oh, I agree. It's just that Jason invited him to dinner tonight."

"Jason? Why would he? Oh, he doesn't know."

"Right."

Dena sighed. "Jason has a very open heart to so many. He's so much like his father in that respect. They see a man in need, and they reach out and go the distance, plus some, to help. I guess Jason saw that need in Mr. Black."

"Yeah. Krispin asked if I had a problem with him coming to church. I told him it was a free country. But I wanted to tell him to go someplace else. I'm not very loving, am I?"

"You're being cautious. I tell you what, if Mr. Black comes to church, why don't you sit with your father and me?"

"I might just do that."

"Good. Now it's time to get back to the family. Clear your head, say a prayer, give yourself a moment, then come back and join us. By the way, I think Brianne's pregnant again. She's looking awfully pale. But they haven't said anything yet."

Jess chuckled. "You get pleasure out of that, don't you?"

Dena laughed. "Not that she's sick but that I have another grandbaby on the way, you betcha. Another one to love and spoil and let the parents do the raising."

"What about when it's my turn?"

"Oh, honey, I'll love your children just as much as I love my other grandchildren. You're so much a part of my family I can't imagine you not being here."

"Thanks, Mom. That means the world to me."

"Terry blew it last week?"

"Afraid so, but she doesn't have a clue. She loves her family, but there really isn't room in her life for me at this time. Maybe someday. I have the mother I never had; my life is full."

Dena hugged her. "I love you, sweetheart. Remember, when all is said and done, your father and I love you very much."

"I know, and I appreciate it."

Dena smiled and winked. No words were spoken, but Jess knew Dena saw into her heart, her longing to be a wife and a mother, to have her own family one day. "It'll happen, Jess. Trust the Lord."

Jess sniffed. "I am."

Dena gave Jess a kiss on the cheek and left her to finish putting her emotions back in place. *Thank You for my family. For Dena, she's such a special gift, Lord, to Dad and to me.* Jess paused, then asked, *What's going on with Krispin Black?*

❧

Krispin found himself aware of Jess in the congregation but refused to give her more than a passing thought. Instead he prayed for her on a regular basis. She seemed relaxed enough when he walked past her and nodded hello.

It had been three weeks since the family dinner invitation from Pastor Russell. And they had had three more discipleship meetings. Pastor Russell wanted him to become part of the mentor program in the church, where they teamed up seasoned Christians with new converts. The available men at this time were Wayne Kearns, Jordan Lamont and a Greg Steadman. Krispin had been praying over the choices. He liked Jordan, but his baby was due in the next few weeks. Wayne seemed like a silly idea, being Jess's father. So Krispin settled on Greg Steadman. Greg was also a lobsterman and had a wife and six kids. They were hard-working people, and Krispin was sure Greg didn't understand business. Not that Greg needed to, since he worked for one of the larger fishing companies. He sometimes went out for weeks at a time, which was a drawback for being Krispin's mentor, but Pastor Russell explained that those long sea voyages happened during the winter months, not the summer.

So Krispin found himself pacing back and forth in his shop, waiting on Greg Steadman, his mentor. The old wooden planks that made up the flooring were thick and uneven from years of use.

The large door creaked open. A man with burly shoulders and a huge brown beard stood in the doorway. "You Krispin?"

"Yes, are you Greg Steadman?"

"Ayup!"

Krispin wanted to groan. Greg seemed to be your stereotypical Maine fisherman. "Come on in. The AC is on."

"Feels like it. Whatcha working on?"

"I'm trying to make an ocean kayak using strips of wood."

"A strip-built kayak—awesome. Got some plans?"

"Yes, over there."

Greg walked over to the makeshift table of a couple of sawhorses and a sheet of marine plywood. "Sweet. Ever build one before?"

"Nope, have you?"

"Nope, but I've wanted to. Mind if I lend you a hand?"

"That would be wonderful. I'm still learning how to use these tools."

Greg scanned the workbench. "Nice tools. All new?"

"Afraid so."

"Hey, don't apologize. So what would you like to ask me?"

"I don't know. I guess the first question is how does this mentor thing work?"

Greg sat down and brushed his beard with his hand. "I've found that the best way to approach this is to start by being friends, and through the friendship, you'll have the freedom to ask me questions. I'll challenge you from time to time on your prayer life, scripture reading, and attendance in church, if necessary, but the key is honesty between us. If I can't make a meeting, I'll be frank with you. I have six children, a wife, and things come up. Not to mention work. My summers aren't as busy. I want you to be totally honest with me, as well. Can you do that?"

"Yes, I think so. Am I supposed to tell you all my sins?"

"No. You're welcome to tell me anything you need to discuss. But I don't need a biography. Pastor says you're a computer programmer who writes encryption codes. And until recently you owned a part of a company."

"Yes. I started writing programs when I was twelve."

"Man, I could never have done that. Math and me never got along real well. My daughter, Lissa, she's a snap at it. She's nine and my oldest."

"Has she been tested?"

"Ayup. The school said she scored a ninth-grade level in the third grade. How is that possible?"

"It's possible. I started algebra when I was in the fourth grade."

"Do you think Lissa should be taking algebra next year?"

"Only if she wants to. On the other hand, private lessons might be better. It was really hard on me in school to be an overachiever. The other kids weren't as excited about my math as I or the teachers were."

"I wouldn't want to have her picked on in school." Greg looked back at the tools. "So tell me why you're building a kayak. To replace the one Jess Kearns ran over?"

Krispin let out a nervous chuckle. "Yes and no. I need something different to work on. I don't know if woodworking will do it, but I'm burnt out with computer programming. Don't get me wrong, I still can do it. I just don't have the passion for it that I once did. After I achieved all that I set out to, I felt empty."

"Ah, I hear ya. That's when you started searching for the answers to life and found the Lord, right?"

"Yes, but that hasn't totally changed how I feel about my work."

"Well, my daddy always said a man can't do much better than to work with his hands. At the end of the day, he has something to show for all his hard work. I think woodworking might just be the ticket. I'm no craftsman with woodworking, but I can saw a straight line and use a router and a few of the other tools you've purchased. Would you like some help?"

"That would be wonderful, yes. I do believe I could use your help."

"Great. I'll come around nine tomorrow morning, and we can get started. What do you want to learn first?"

"The table saw, then the planer."

"Not a problem." Greg looked over at the wood. "Just how many kayaks do you plan on making?"

"One."

Greg whistled. "Do you know you have enough wood for two, possibly three?"

Krispin chuckled. "I figured I'd make a lot of mistakes."

"Ah. Makes sense. Okay, I'll see you in the morning." And just like that, Greg Steadman left. Krispin sat down on the stool and replayed the entire conversation. Greg was an interesting guy. There was more to him than his rough exterior would suggest.

"I think I'm going to like working with him, Lord. He's down to earth and a straight shooter. Something I haven't had a lot of experience with in the business world. Thanks for sending a man who's going to stretch me."

❧

Jess flew through the house, looking for her binoculars. Krispin Black was holed up in one of the old warehouses on the other side of the harbor. She hadn't been sure she'd seen him going in and out of the old building a couple times, but today she could see his Mustang outside and knew he was there. What he was doing? She didn't have a clue, but she wanted to find out.

It made no sense, him wanting to live in Squabbin Bay. And while he'd been right, it wasn't her business to know what he was doing here, she certainly couldn't just sit by and wait. What was her obsession with this man? The fact that she nearly killed him made her feel like she had a certain responsibility toward him, which was foolish, or so she told herself over and over again.

She had no business spying on him. She stopped looking for the binoculars and sat down in the easy chair in the living room. Her Bible was on the side table. She pulled it into her lap and started to read.

Father God, why is Krispin Black living in Squabbin Bay? She paused long enough to wait for an answer, hoping she'd hear God's voice on this. Instead she looked down at her open Bible and found a verse she read many times before. Jeremiah 29:13: *"You will seek me and find me when you seek me with all your heart."*

Father, have I not given You all of my heart? Is this why I'm so bothered by Krispin's presence in town?

Lord, what is in my heart that I haven't given over to You? I've confessed my attraction to Krispin. I know he's not saved, and I won't get involved with him. Are my feelings for Krispin keeping me from giving You all my heart? Lord, I'm afraid of him. I'm afraid of my reactions to him. He seems so different. Is it my fault? Did the accident cause this change in him?

"Oh, Lord, forgive me for not trusting You with Krispin. Help me get over my obsession with him."

"Jess?"

Jess turned to see Randi standing at her back door with her hand on her protruding stomach. "Jess, help me, please."

Jess jumped up. "What's the matter?"

"I think I'm in labor."

"Oh no!" Jess ran to the back door and helped her best friend in. "What happened?"

Randi chuckled. "What do you mean, what happened?"

"I'm sorry. Why do you think you're in labor?"

Randi's body convulsed.

"Oh dear, don't worry. I'll call Jordan. Where is he?"

"In Boston."

"You've got to be kidding!"

Randi shook her head. Jess rolled her eyes heavenward, grabbed the phone, and called the fire department. Then she left a message on Jordan's cell phone and called Randi's parents. Jordan's return call came in at the same time Randi's parents and the ambulance arrived. Randi held on to Jess. "Jess, you've got to come with me. I need a coach."

"Randi, I'm no coach."

"You're the closest thing I've got. Stay with me, please."

"Okay, but only until Jordan gets back." *Lord, help Jordan get back in time.*

Randi's water broke, and Jess nearly fainted. *O Lord, help me. There's no way I'll make it through this.* Randi squeezed Jess's arm. "Help me breathe, Jess."

"Breathe? Oh, you mean like those prenatal breathing exercises."

Randi nodded. Jess held on to Randi's hand. Together they breathed the first level of Lamaze breathing technique. She remembered the second level, but the third and fourth totally escaped her memory. Frankly, she hadn't paid that much attention when Randi had showed them to her when she and Jordan were taking the prenatal classes.

Josie Smith took Randi's pulse and other vitals. "When is your due date, Randi?"

"End of August."

"Guess this little one doesn't want to wait." Josie smiled. "You're doing fine. I need to check the dilation."

Randi nodded. Jess's eyes widened, then she turned to the gathering crowd. "Everyone out, now!" Jess demanded.

Josie and Randi chuckled. Josie added, "It's her first. Trust me, I've delivered quite a few little ones over the years. You're doing fine, Randi."

"Thanks, Josie."

"Where's Jordan?" Josie asked while doing the examination. "Three centimeters. You've got some time."

Randi let out a pent-up breath. "Thanks. He's in Boston. We thought we had enough time."

"Apparently the little one wants to see her or his mommy and daddy now." Josie covered Randi, then removed her plastic gloves.

"What's wrong with Jess?" Jess heard a winded male voice call out.

"Ain't Jess; it's Randi. She's having a baby," someone from the crowd called out.

"Oh," he mumbled. At that point Jess recognized the voice of Krispin Black. "Where's Jordan?"

"Boston," said another.

"Where are they taking Randi?" Krispin asked again.

"Blue Hill Hospital in Ellsworth, most likely." Jess couldn't help but notice Krispin's curiosity in this entire event.

"Jessss!" Randi cried out.

"I'm here, Randi. I'm here." Jess held on to Randi's hand and followed the EMTs out the door and into the ambulance. Krispin was on his cell phone as she got in. *That's odd. Who would he be telling?*

seven

Krispin walked away from Jess's house as they wheeled Randi into the ambulance. "Jordan, it's me, Krispin Black. I imagine you're trying to get home for Randi right away."

"Yeah, how'd you know? Never mind. It's Squabbin Bay."

"Right. Look, I have a friend who owns a chopper and lives in Boston. Would you like me to call him?"

"Yes."

"Okay, I'll call you right back." Krispin clicked through the address book on his phone, found Michael James's private phone number, and dialed. A few minutes later Krispin had the location and directions finalized with Michael. Krispin called Jordan and passed on the information.

"Thanks, Krispin. I appreciate it."

"No problem. I'll take care of the fuel expense, unless you barter with Michael for some photos. He's always needing some promotional shots."

"All right, thanks again."

"As a favor to me, I doubt Michael will even bother charging you, but I've always offered."

"Gotcha. I'll see you later. Thanks again, Krispin."

"You're welcome." Krispin headed back to his shop. He wanted to go to the hospital and wait to hear how Randi was doing but knew it wasn't his place. He'd have to wait in town like most of the folks around here.

Greg was leaning against the doorframe. "So what happened?"

"I'm sorry I'm late. Randi Lamont went into labor."

Greg chuckled. "I know that. You forget we live in a very small town. I also heard you called out wondering what happened to Jess. What's going on with you two?"

64

"Nothing. I'm not worthy of her."

"Worthy?"

"Yeah. You know some of my past. Well, when it comes to women, I've had more than my share. According to God, a lot more. Anyway, I don't think I have the right to consider marriage when I've messed up so badly and hurt so many."

"Hmm, so how do you see Jess?"

"She's pure, untouched by the world. She deserves better than me."

Greg chuckled. "Well that's probably true, but you're missing a point."

"What?"

"You're redeemed. As in you've been forgiven of all the wrong things you've done. You stand before God as one free from the past because you've repented and given your past to God."

"I know, but—"

"Ain't no buts about it. You're redeemed, same as she. So tell me again why you can't have a relationship with Jess?"

"You mean besides the fact that she nearly killed me the first time we met?"

Greg roared with laughter. "Yeah, besides that. Oh, and the fact that she saved your life."

Krispin laughed. "That, too." He walked over to his table saw. "You said you'd teach me how to use this today."

"Fair enough, but you and Jess is not a closed subject."

"It is if I'm not ready to talk about it."

"I'll give ya that." Greg joined him at the table saw. "You see this plate?" He pointed to the small plate that had a long, narrow slit where the blade came through. "If we remove it, like this, we have access to remove and tighten a blade."

Greg continued the demonstration, and by the end of the day, Krispin was cutting, raising, and lowering the blade and knew just about every piece of the saw. He found Greg to be a good teacher—patient, never belittling him for what he didn't know. Which was quite a lot. He only knew which tools to buy because of the various articles he'd read online and from the kayak-building forum where folks listed the tools they used for their projects.

"Tomorrow we'll work on the planer. All this wood needs to be planed to the same size."

"Right." Krispin looked over at the rectangular frame. He'd assembled it but didn't have a clue as to how it worked. He knew he would put the boards in one way, and it would automatically feed them out the other side, but how the blades were to be set, he didn't know. Tonight he'd read up on the instruction manual for the planer and the router. Both needed to be learned.

Greg left, and Krispin cleaned up the sawdust from all the cutting he'd done. He liked the feel of the wood in his hands and the various textures of the different kinds of wood.

The door creaked open. Without turning, Krispin asked, "Did you forget something?"

"Not exactly." Jess's voice resounded in his ears.

"Jess. I'm sorry, I thought you were someone else."

"I gathered. What are you doing in here?"

"Cleaning up." He knew it was a glib answer, but he really preferred that she stayed on her side of Squabbin Bay and not his. "How's Randi?"

A sweet smile rose on her lips. Krispin turned back to sweeping up the sawdust.

"Randi is fine. Jordan arrived in time to relieve me. I've never been so grateful. Having babies is messy business."

"I wouldn't know myself, but I'm glad I'm a man. Has the baby arrived?" Krispin dumped the full dustpan into the garbage can.

"Not yet. The doctor said it could still take some time." Jess walked around the room. "What are you building?"

"A kayak, I hope."

She glanced over at the pile of wood. "You have enough

material here for several."

"I figure I'm going to be making a lot of mistakes."

"Ah. Krispin, I need to know why you're here. I know it probably is none of my business. . . ."

Krispin put the dustpan and broom aside. "Jess, I will leave town if you're that uncomfortable with me living here."

"As much as I'd love to say yes to your leaving town, it isn't my place to do so. I'm thinking we should talk a bit, maybe get to know one another."

"Why are you so uncomfortable around me?"

She leveled a gaze at him that would have tumbled a brick-yard with its intensity. And he understood it had been his forward nature and rude comments. "Jess, I promise never to speak that way to you again. I was out of line, completely out of line. I'd like to say I was out of my mind. But I wasn't. I'd become a man who thought mostly of myself. Please forgive me."

She paused for a moment, then released her gaze. "All right. But it will be awhile before I can trust you."

"I understand."

"You're letting your hair grow out?"

Krispin shrugged his shoulders. "I guess. I've kept it so short for business. I figured I could skip seeing the barber for a couple months."

"It looks like it's going to come in curly."

Krispin chuckled. "You don't know the meaning of my name, do you?"

"Afraid not. What is it?"

" 'Curly hair.' The way my mother tells it, she and Dad took one look at my full head of curly hair and named me Krispin. Before I was born, they were planning on naming me Walter."

"Krispin is much better."

"Thanks. I've been happy with it. It's unique, and because of that, I think it's helped give me an edge in business."

"Speaking of business, don't you have a partnership in a company?"

"*Had.* I sold out."

"Why?"

Krispin fought the desire to tell her he'd become a Christian. Jess needed to see the change in him before he told her. *Actions speak louder than words,* his father always said. "Let's just say, I wasn't very happy with my life."

"Secrets?"

"Omissions."

Jess pouted. She had a beautiful pout, he decided. "Well, I'm going home. I've got to lock up now."

"Oh, sorry." Jess bolted toward the door. "Krispin, why did you come running over to my place when you saw the ambulance?"

"I'd hate to have anything bad happen to my rescuer," he admitted.

"You seem different." Jess reached for the door.

"I am. And I think it's for the good."

Jess gave a slight nod of the head. "Yeah, I like this new you much better than the one I pulled out of the harbor."

Krispin smiled and fought off the desire to say, *I aim to please,* knowing it would make him look superficial in her eyes. But he did want to please Jess. His prayers for her grew with intensity each passing day. He'd fallen in love with Jess—no longer with the vile selfishness of his past but with a healthy respect for her and a desire to see her succeed. He wanted to ask her out to dinner but knew she'd take the invitation the wrong way. Instead he simply said, "Good night, Jess."

"Night, Krispin."

&

The next morning Jess got up thirty minutes earlier to gather in the lobsters. By midmorning she was done. She went home, showered, and drove to the hospital to meet Randi and Jordan's little one. The joy on the parents' faces was so contagious Jess also beamed. "She's beautiful," Jess whispered.

"Yeah, she is." Jordan clicked off a couple of pictures of Jess, Randi, and Ella Ruth, Squabbin Bay's newest resident.

"Would you like to hold her?" Randi offered.

"Love to. Do I need to put on a gown or something?"

"No, just wash your hands; that will be fine." Randi handed her daughter over to Jess with a gentle kiss on the forehead.

Jess cradled the tiny bundle in her arms. "I don't think I've ever held someone so tiny."

A long moment of silence filled the room, broken only by Jordan's clicking of the camera. "How do you put up with that?"

Randi laughed. "I'm still getting used to it."

"It looks like she'll have Randi's dark eyes." Jordan beamed. "See how black the irises are?"

Randi had a very unique characteristic in her nearly black eyes. And Jess knew that Jordan had always been fascinated by them. They reminded him of his Native American great-grandmother. "They're beautiful."

"Mom said my eyes were black when I was first born, too," Randi admitted.

Ella Ruth started to squirm. Her little fists poked out of the blanket. Her face scrunched up, and a little yelp came out.

"Must be feeding time." Jess handed the baby back to Randi. "She's very beautiful. You guys must be so pleased."

"The Lord's blessed us. She's fine. They're watching her bilirubin count to make sure her liver is working fine, but all indications are that she'll be able to leave the hospital with Randi tomorrow."

Jess stayed a few minutes longer. But Ella Ruth was hungry, so Jess left to allow Randi to breastfeed her baby.

The desire to have her own little one occupied her thoughts on the drive home. She'd never been one to ooh and ahh over an infant, but this one hit closer to home. Her best friend was now a mother. Jess didn't even have a prospect for a husband.

She went to the office and worked on co-op business until old Ben Costa came in. "Hey there, Jess. Is your dad around?" Ben had retired a couple years ago, but he kept his boat and a couple pots just to keep himself busy.

"I believe he's out at the old Ford place. What's up?"

"Nothin' really. Just saw your grandpa in town, and I wanted to make sure he was aware."

Jess sighed. Her grandfather's summer of stealing the other lobstermen's lobsters had been hardest on her father, but Ben had suffered a lot, too. Even worse, that same summer, a couple of teens running fast and loose had set his house on fire. Then old Ben himself had left his cigar burning and the gas on in his boat, and he had lost that, as well. Thankfully, Ben's insurance covered a large portion of his losses. "We know. Daddy has Grandpa and Grandma living at the house with them."

"Has he been able to kick that nasty habit?"

"Yes. Grandpa goes to Gamblers Anonymous regularly, and Grandma takes care of the finances."

"Good. Your grandpa was a good man. Nothing like sin to cloud a man's judgment. Well, that's all. I just wanted to be sure."

"No problem, Ben. Come by any time."

Ben waved as he shuffled down the steps. For a man in his seventies, he was spry enough. Jess noticed he held the railing tightly as he took each step. At the same time, she noticed Krispin Black walking into the Dockside Grill. She wondered if he ever cooked for himself. She'd seen him many times coming out of the restaurant with a meal to go.

Jess looked back at the quarterlies. The income this year was better than last. The number of lobsters harvested was a bit more, but not too much more. One thing Jess had learned early on was not to glut the market with too much lobster.

Mark Bisbee ran the warehouse for the co-op. Jess placed a call to him. "Hi, Mark. How's it going?"

"Fine, fine. Orders are coming in steady. And so far we've had enough lobster to meet the needs."

"Wonderful. Did you receive the order I faxed from the Weathervane Restaurants?"

"Ayup, got it right here. You gave them a mighty nice price."

"Yeah, we'll lose a nickel a lobster, but I think the size of the order will keep us in the black."

"No doubt. They have restaurants in three states now, and they're still growing. They like getting the freshest lobsters they can."

"And we aim to please. Thanks, Mark. Keep me posted."

"Will do. Talk with you later. Bye."

Jess listened to the disconnection hum for a moment, then placed the phone back in its holder. With her work done, she looked out at the harbor. The ocean was calm. The prospect of paddling her kayak through the waters seemed like a good idea. She locked up the office and ran over to the boathouse where she and her father stored their kayaks along with all their fishing equipment during the summer months. Within minutes she was dressed in her wetsuit and carrying her kayak over her head to the small dock.

Once inside, she paddled her way through the harbor and over to Krispin's warehouse. She pulled the boat up onto the small dock outside his building and knocked on the seaside door.

A moment later, Greg Steadman appeared. "Hi, Jess. What can I do you for?"

"Uh, I was looking for Krispin."

"He's here. Hang on."

Greg slipped behind the gray weathered boards that made

up the door. A couple of minutes later, Krispin appeared. "Hi, Jess. What's up?"

"I thought maybe you'd like to go kayaking with me. But I see you're busy."

"Afraid so. Greg's teaching me how to use a router."

"Ah. Well, I won't keep you. See you around." Jess headed back to her kayak.

"Jess?"

Jess turned back.

"Thanks for the offer. Maybe some other time."

"Of course."

Why, why, why, did I do that? He's going to think I'm chasing him now. Stupid! Stupid! Stupid!

Jess worked her way out of the harbor and to a small island that she and Randi used to play on when they were younger. They had made a small hut out of driftwood. Jess found the remains of a childhood castle and the makings of a new fort by some other child. Upon closer inspection, some of the missing wood had come from their castle. Jess smiled.

She sat down on a rock and drew in the sand with a stick. She wasn't a child any longer. The days of kings and queens, princes and princesses were long gone. She was a woman, alone in this world. Alone for the very first time. She scanned the harbor. Boats of all different shapes and sizes painted the horizon. She knew most of the people on those vessels, so why did she feel so alone?

Her father was married now. Her best friend was married and had a baby. The co-op didn't demand every waking minute she had, and even lobstering only took up a small amount of her time each day. She was bored. Alone and bored was not a good combination in Squabbin Bay.

Was it time to send out her résumé again? Was it time to go back to corporate America and enter the business she'd gone to school for?

The co-op still needed her, she argued. She had a place in

Squabbin Bay. So why was she so uncomfortable here now?

The ever so delightful image of Krispin Black flooded her senses. *Lord, it isn't fair. Why am I attracted to men who don't put You first in their lives?*

eight

Krispin watched Jess paddle away. *Why does she keep coming around?*

"Penny for your thoughts?"

Startled, Krispin turned back toward Greg. "Sorry."

"What's the matter, Krispin? Have you not forgiven yourself?"

"It's not that. I've been trying real hard to avoid Jessica Kearns. And now she's stopping by. Why would she do that?"

Greg chuckled. "Oh, I don't know. Maybe she likes you."

"She's afraid of me."

"Pardon?"

Krispin sighed, then filled Greg in on his and Jess's conversation yesterday.

"So let me get this straight. You promised not to say or do anything crude, rude, or socially unacceptable to her, and you're confused by her appearance here this morning?"

Krispin nodded.

"Seems obvious to me. She's attracted to you."

"But—"

Greg raised one of his beefy fingers. "You're redeemed, Krispin. But if you were as rude as you said you were, I imagine your bigger problem will be getting past her father."

Krispin plopped down on a stool. Going head to head with Wayne Kearns, confessing his sin toward his daughter, struck him as both undesirable and impossible.

"Tell ya what. I'm going to go home now. Give this matter some prayer and thought. Wayne has a real talent with wood. You might want to ask for his help."

Krispin shook his head no. "I asked for you to be my mentor."

"I wasn't saying I'd stop being your mentor. You're a good man, Krispin. Your heart has changed since the day of the accident. Relax and give yourself a break. I'll see you tomorrow."

Greg left without a further word. Krispin sat in a quandary. He liked Jess. No, he loved Jess. But he had to admit he didn't feel good enough for her. Compounding the problem, he respected Wayne. What father would want to know the unholy thoughts a man has entertained or, in his case, said to his daughter? Yet was it the right course of action? Should he apologize to Wayne? Should he seek Wayne's blessing to pursue a relationship with Jess? Should he even consider a relationship with Jess?

Yesterday he thought they could be friends. Today the very thought of it scared him.

He spent the next few minutes in prayer, then closed up the shop and went home. What he didn't expect to see was Wayne Kearns's truck in his driveway. His posture was noticeably rigid.

"Mr. Kearns."

"Mr. Black," Wayne's voice strained.

"What can I do for you?"

"I want to know what kind of a game you're playing with my daughter, Mr. Black. You've seemed to convince Pastor Russell you're a changed man, but frankly, I don't see it."

Krispin sighed. "What exactly are you not sure of? Would you like to go inside while we talk?"

Wayne nodded. "Look, I'm sure you're a good enough person. You did drop the lawsuit. . . ."

"I never filed one," Krispin interjected.

"Right. Okay, but why did you come to Squabbin Bay?"

Krispin let out a nervous chuckle and held the door open to his cottage. "Because of you."

"Me?"

"Yeah. It's a long story. Well, perhaps not that long. But

would you like a soft drink or something?"

"Sure. Got any beer?"

"No. You drink beer?"

"No, but I was checking if you did."

"Ah." Krispin held the door of the refrigerator open. "Here ya go. You're free to search my cabinets, too. Now if you'd come at the time of the accident, that would be a different story."

"Gotcha. Let's sit down, Mr. Black."

They went into the living room. Wayne sat on the couch with his legs spread and elbows resting on his knees. "Jason says you've prayed for salvation. Why?"

"Because I came to realize I wasn't happy with my life. I've had fortune and fame, as they say. Although my fame is really in the work I've done, but I've lived a lifestyle that was very worldly. Things came easy for me. . .too easy. But I was empty. And my short time in Squabbin Bay showed me another side of life, the ability to be content with little, to enjoy who and where you are. And frankly, your words drove me to reconsider my life."

Wayne relaxed. "So you've really given your life to the Lord?"

"Yes, sir. You can ask Greg Steadman. He's my mentor, and he's been helping me in the shop."

Wayne smiled. "I already spoke with Greg."

Krispin knitted his eyebrows. "Then why—"

"I'm a father concerned for his daughter. Jess shared with Dena, and I know you propositioned her on more than one occasion."

Krispin felt his face grow hot with humiliation. "I'm really sorry. I was totally out of line."

"Yes, you were."

"Mr. Kearns, I am attracted to Jess. But I don't want a woman in my life right now. I don't think I can handle it."

Krispin felt the weight of Wayne's scrutinizing gaze.

"I think you may be right."

Krispin relaxed.

"What is the status of your relationship with Jess?"

"Nothing more than casual friends, if that."

"Mr. Black, I'm not blind. I saw Jess at your warehouse yesterday and then again today with her kayak. And the whole town is buzzing about how you ran over to her place, concerned that something had happened to Jess when Randi went into labor."

Krispin bent his head low and collected his thoughts. "Jess came to me yesterday and today. The concern for her welfare is genuine. I do care for her. But as I said, I don't think it is wise for me to be considering having a relationship. I want to get my life right with the Lord first. *And I'm still not confident that God would allow me to have a wife*, he silently added. "Also, I told Jess I'd leave town if it was too uncomfortable having me live here."

"I see. Let's talk about that. If you came here to try and refocus your life, have you done that? I accept your confession in believing in Jesus Christ now, but is that all you needed to accomplish by coming to Squabbin Bay?"

Krispin had given this a lot of thought. "Mr. Kearns, can I be perfectly honest with you?"

Wayne nodded.

Krispin poured out his heart—his fears, his frustrations, the things he'd been learning and reevaluating in his life, everything that had been spinning in his mind for the past year and especially during the three months since the accident.

"Krispin, you've come a long way. I'm happy for you. But you must realize you're not the only person who's led the kind of life you did before you got saved. I myself was no gem. God forgives completely. You need to forgive yourself."

"Greg said something very similar."

"If you like, you can feel free to call me if you're dealing with any serious temptations."

Krispin's face reddened.

"It's Jess, isn't it?"

Krispin swallowed. "Yes."

"When Dena and I first started to get to know one another, we dealt with some strong emotions waking up in both of us. You should do just fine if you give the matter to the Lord and give it a lot of prayer. He'll help, trust me. I know from firsthand experience."

Krispin felt even more embarrassed, if that were possible. "I don't know if Jess feels the same way about me. We hardly know one another."

"Trust the Lord. If He's designed the two of you for marriage to one another, then it will happen. If not, He'll give you the strength to get past your affections for her right now."

"How can you be so blunt about this? It's your daughter we're speaking about."

"It is my daughter, but I learned not too long ago I had to trust her to make the right choice, and so far, she has.

"Now, tell me about the strip-line kayak you're building with Greg."

And just like that the subject changed. Krispin decided he liked Wayne Kearns and respected him even more.

❧

The following day, Jess sat down at her computer and punched in her password. Something was wrong. She opened her e-mail. It had been downloaded recently. The fine hairs on the back of her neck began to tingle.

Jess's hand shook. This computer was tied into the co-op's computer. Someone must have been on her computer. Why? She looked over the various files. She gathered the backup disks from the past three months, then called Randi.

"Hey, Randi, how are you? How's the baby?"

"We're both doing well. It will take a bit to get used to no sleep, though."

"I've heard that. Hey, I hate to cut this short, but I'm in a bit of a jam here, and I'm wondering if you can help me out." Jess went on to explain.

"First, call the sheriff. Second, call Krispin. He's an encryption software genius of some sort. He doesn't know it, but I checked into him. He's considered an expert in the field."

"Really?"

"Yup, and I'm sure he can tell you how your system was breached and how to fix it."

"All right. Do you have his phone number?"

"Sure, hang on." Randi was gone from the phone for a moment. "Here ya go." She gave Jess his home and cell phone numbers.

"Thanks, Randi."

"You're welcome. I think it's probably a couple of local kids. But still, you can't allow anyone to break into your system like that."

"Right. I'll talk with you later. 'Bye."

Jess hung up and called the sheriff, then left a message on Krispin's cell phone to come to the co-op as soon as possible. She headed to the office to check the computers at the co-op.

She was surprised to see Krispin Black waiting outside the office when she arrived.

"Hi, Jess. What's the problem?"

"Randi says you're an encryption expert."

"I write encryption software. Why?"

"I think someone broke into my home computer."

"Oh boy, any money missing?" Krispin asked.

"As best as I could tell, no. Can you help?"

"I can try. First, do you have backup copies?"

"Right here." She lifted the small bundle of disks.

"Good, let's get to work." He held the door open and let her pass.

Jess watched as Krispin fired up the computer. Within

minutes, he had a bunch of numerals and digits that didn't make any sense to her. Jess left him to do his job and went to the desk to sort through the mail.

"Morning, Jess. What seems to be the problem?" Sheriff McKean said as he entered the co-op.

"I think someone broke into my home computer."

"Interesting. How do you know this?"

"My e-mail had been downloaded when I wasn't home. Krispin's looking on the office computer to see if anyone's tampered with them."

"All right. Keep me posted on Krispin's discoveries. He is qualified, right?"

"According to Randi, yes."

"Good enough for me. I'll see you later."

Three hours later, Krispin got up from the computer. "Jess, you're fine. I only saw remote access from your home computer, nothing else."

"What time? Can you tell that?"

"Not with this software. I've uploaded a better encryption software package and changed all your access passwords. You can change them again after I leave." Krispin handed her a small piece of paper.

"If anyone got in, it would have been through that computer. Do you keep your doors locked?"

"No. I guess I should, huh?"

"If you're going to have access from your home computer to this one, yes. However, I'll need to encrypt your home computer, as well. At the moment, no one can enter this computer without your permission, and that means even looking at pop-up windows on the Internet."

"How much do I owe you?"

"Nothing. It's my own program; not even my company had access to this one. However, the password is twenty-five digits. You'll need to keep the key handy but in a safe place."

"Twenty-five?"

"I can reduce it, but until we find out who's trying to get in, I felt higher encryption would be wiser."

"You're right. Sorry."

"Also, I cleaned up your hard drive. You should notice it running faster." Krispin smiled.

"You're good at this, aren't you?"

"I have a knack."

Jess laughed. "I'd say that was an understatement. Okay, why don't I take you to my house and I'll fix us some lunch while you work on my home computer?"

"I'd love to, but it will have to be later. I have an appointment for lunch."

"Sure, just let me know when, and I'll work around your schedule."

Krispin placed his hand on the doorknob. "Thanks for calling me, Jess. I'm glad I was able to help."

"Thanks for coming. I was so scared someone got into the financial records or even to the bank account information."

"You're safe now. But you might want to speak with the bank and change your account information, just as an extra precaution. They can give you a new account number in no time and transfer the funds over."

"I'll go to the bank right away. Thanks again, Krispin."

"You're welcome." Krispin left and went to his car.

Jess watched with interest. He seemed more confident today. As if things were falling into place for him. Jess prayed a short prayer of thanks for Krispin and asked the Lord to continue to draw Krispin close to Him.

❧

Krispin hurried over to the shop and met Greg just as he was about to pull out of the parking lot. "Hey, sorry about that, Greg. Jess had an issue with her computer."

"No problem. The wife's looking forward to meeting you. I hope you like lobster salad."

Krispin smiled. "Yes." Whenever he did leave Squabbin

Bay, he probably wouldn't be eating lobster for two years.

"Great, 'cause she made minestrone soup."

Krispin roared. "Thanks."

"I remembered you said you liked it well enough but it wasn't your all-time favorite food."

"Touché."

"Follow me."

Krispin settled back behind the wheel and followed Greg in his old pickup truck. They passed through town and drove out past a huge field peppered with boulders. Greg's home was set back in the woods and up a windy dirt road. Krispin would have to wash and wax his car this weekend.

Pine trees lined the path. A two-story clapboard house painted white with blue trim spread across the clearing. Kids' toys littered the front yard. A couple of bicycles leaned against the front steps. No one would doubt a truckload of children lived in this house.

Their home was humble but clean. The kids were bright, and Lissa, Greg's oldest, knew her math just like her father had said. Bryan, Greg's seven-year-old son, brought in a boat he'd made from a couple of pieces of wood. "See, it floats, too," he boasted.

"Wow, that's great. Maybe you can come and give your dad and me a hand at the shop."

"Really?" Bryan turned toward his father. "Can I, Dad?"

"Since it's all right with Mr. Black, then maybe someday. You need to mind your mother."

"Yes, sir." Bryan ran off to play with the others.

"Mr. Black, can you show me how to do algebra?" Lissa asked.

"Now kids, give Mr. Black some space. Lissa, he's here for lunch, not to be your math tutor."

"Sorry, Daddy."

"I'll be happy to show her a few things. Does she have a book?"

Lissa pulled out a book from under her chair. "Right here. Mommy got it from the library for me after Daddy told her that it was all right for me to learn algebra."

Krispin chuckled. "Okay, how about after lunch? I'll spend a few minutes with you before I go."

"Thank you, Mr. Black. That would be awesome."

Jayne, Greg's wife, set a bowl of minestrone soup and some homemade rolls of Portuguese sweet bread beside him. "Thank you, Jayne. You don't know how good it is to have a home-cooked meal."

"You're not a cook, Mr. Black?"

"Call me Krispin, and no, I'm not."

"I thought most men were these days." She served Greg, then the children, then herself. *The perfect hostess,* he mused.

"I never had time for it. I ordered out a lot. But in Squabbin Bay, take-out eateries are limited."

Jayne laughed. "That's stating it mildly. It took me a few years to adjust to life up here."

"Where were you from?"

"I met Greg in college. I grew up near Hartford, Connecticut."

"A city girl."

Jayne giggled. "Not anymore. I've been countrified, as they like to say."

The meal progressed with light chatter. They were a happy family. After the meal, Krispin sat down with Lissa and helped her to understand the first chapter. Doing the algebraic problems wasn't difficult, but helping her understand concepts behind how to use the math problems took a bit longer than he expected. On the other hand, she was only nine years old and had an incredible mind for mathematics.

He returned to town and went over to the co-op to see if this was a good time for him to work on Jess's computer. It was a typical Northeastern-type cottage that had been converted to a place of business, with grayed weathered shingles and white trim paint around the windows. It had been built into the side of the cliff overlooking the harbor.

Krispin got out of his car and strolled up the walkway to the open front door. Jess stood face-to-face with a stranger, medium build and brown hair. As Krispin watched, the man leaned over and kissed Jess.

"Jess?" Krispin's heart stopped.

nine

"Krispin," Jess gasped. "Trevor, back off."

"Come on, Jess. I'm sorry. Please say you'll get back with me," Trevor pleaded.

"No. Now back off!"

"You heard the lady," Krispin said in a firm voice.

"Is he the reason you won't get back together with me?" Trevor demanded but took a couple steps away from her. Jess had never been so happy to see Krispin.

"Mr. Black and I are friends."

"Right, and I was born yesterday."

"Trev, it's over. It has been for over a year, so why are you here? Never mind, I don't want to know. Go back home to Boston, Trev."

Krispin planted his feet and puffed up his chest. Jess saw she had a defender if needed. If anything, dating Trevor had taught her that he had no backbone. He would not go up against Krispin Black or any other man, for that matter.

"I thought—"

Jess stopped him. "It's over, Trev. I don't love you. Go home."

Trevor started to take a step toward her, then cast a second glance at Krispin and headed out the door. "You'll regret this, Jess."

"No, I only regret the time I spent with you," she mumbled after he walked out the door.

"I'm sorry you had to see that," she said, turning to Krispin.

"Who is he?"

"An old boyfriend from college. Thanks for coming when you did. I was about to smack him."

"I'd be happy to oblige."

Jess laughed. "Seriously, I appreciate your coming in when you did."

"Divine intervention," Krispin said and turned to watch Trevor's departure from the door window.

"Is he gone?"

"He's pulling out now."

"Good." Jess crumpled in her seat. "I loved him once."

"What happened, if you don't mind me asking?"

"He wanted me to live in Boston. But it's more than that. He wouldn't get a job out of college. He's been living off his parents ever since. I guess they got wise and kicked him out. He's incredibly lazy. I never saw it when we were in school. He did his schoolwork and even worked a part-time job. I don't know what happened. Once we were out of school, he changed. And to think I almost. . ." Jess let her words trail off. Confessing her past relationship with Trevor to Krispin Black seemed totally inappropriate.

"What?"

"Never mind."

"Right, okay. I came by to see if you wanted me to work on your home computer."

"Yes, that would be great. Let me finish a couple of things; then I'll bring you over to my house."

Krispin sat down and picked up one of the annual reports of the co-op and thumbed through it while she finished off a couple of e-mails.

"I'm ready."

Krispin placed the report back on the small table.

"What do you think?"

"Interesting. So you founded the co-op?"

"Yeah, it's based off of what the cranberry growers did years ago when they formed their co-op."

"It's a sound plan. You might want to consider. . ."

"What?"

"Sorry, force of habit. I don't know your business. I was just thinking speculatively."

"I'm all ears."

"No, Jess. I shouldn't get involved. It's your business, and you're doing a fine job."

"Thanks, that means a lot."

They got in their cars, and Krispin followed Jess. She kept watching her rearview mirror. The man remained a mystery. It took less than ten minutes to get to her place from the co-op. Jess let him inside the cottage, then left to go to the grocery store. "I'll be right back," she called from the door as he settled in at the computer.

⁂

Krispin found the problem. Someone had been on Jess's computer the day before. Whoever it was had made three password attempts before figuring out her password. His thoughts drifted to Trevor. If he was as lazy as Jess said he was, he might have been after some quick cash from Jess.

Krispin looked to see if Jess's bank records had been accessed by her computer yesterday. They had. But by her or the intruder? Krispin got up from the computer and started to pace. He picked up his cell phone and looked at his incoming calls. He called the number that Jess had called from earlier today. The house phone rang. Krispin hung up.

He went back to her computer and found a Trojan program that would silently run in the background and gather all her financial information. It had been installed yesterday. To the best of his knowledge, it hadn't been accessed for its information yet. Krispin deleted the nasty program and installed his encryption program on her computer.

Jess returned. "Hey, how's it going?"

"Jess, someone has been on this computer."

"What?"

"I found evidence they tried three times for your password, then they got into the portal to the co-op's computer. I checked your online banking records. One log-in occurred yesterday. Was that you?"

"No. Wait, yes. Last night."

"Okay, that's the only instance I found. However, as with the co-op's bank account, you should change your account information, as well."

She glanced up at the clock. He did, also. Five of five was too late. "I'll do that first thing tomorrow. I'll have Dad go lobstering in the morning."

"Jess, I don't want to scare you, but you have all your information on this computer. Someone could steal your identity with the information on here."

"I knew I should have bought a Mac."

Krispin laughed. "There is that. However, I've put my encryption program on here and another twenty-five-digit password."

Jess sighed.

"Hey, I could have made it forty-nine digits."

"No way. I'd never use the thing. Please tell me you're just scaring me."

"True, I am scaring you. You could take some simple steps to protect yourself, and you won't need a twenty-five digit password forever. The more difficult encryption is to protect you because someone has tried and succeeded. What I find odd is that nothing is missing. However, I did find a Trojan horse program that would gather all the information they would need, like credit card numbers, bank numbers, your social security number, and things as harmless as your e-mails to your friends. All of that is to say I don't know who is after your information or what information they are after. It could be somebody just after the co-op information. Or it could be more personal. I hate to ask, but is Trevor capable—"

"Trevor? Nah. Well, wait, he does lug his computer around with him everywhere he goes. I thought he was always playing games online, though."

"It might not be him. And if he's after money, why would he have waited, when he had access to your accounts?"

"Because I don't have that much in my account right now."

"Possibly." Krispin tapped the top of the computer. "You're safe for now. Please lock the house when you're gone."

"I will. I promise."

"Good. I'd better be going."

"Krispin, I bought a couple of steaks. Would you like to have dinner with me?"

Krispin paused. He'd love to, but was it wise?

"I want to thank you for all your help."

"Jess, I don't—"

"Shh, I know the fear. I have my own. But we'll sit on the front deck of the house. We'll keep ourselves in view of everyone."

"All right. I have to go home for a few minutes, though. Is that a problem?"

"Not at all. Why don't you come back in an hour? I should have everything done by then."

"Can I bring anything?"

"Not this time. Maybe next."

Krispin left the house and sat behind the wheel of his car, his hands shaking. "Dear Lord, give me strength."

ta

After Krispin left, Jess thought better of the two of them being alone and picked up the phone. "Hey, Mom."

"Hi, Jess, what's up?"

"I need a favor. I've invited Krispin to dinner tonight. He's coming in an hour. I'd like you and Dad to be praying. And could you swing by at around nine? I want the safety check."

"I guess we could. Are you sure you want to do this?"

"Yeah, he's been a huge help today." Jess started to prepare the dinner. "Plus, Trevor came to the co-op today."

"Trevor?"

"Yup. He wanted to get back together."

"Oh, Jess, what did you tell him?"

"Before or after he kissed me?"

"He what?"

Jess sighed. "Mom, I can't believe I loved him. His kiss meant nothing to me. It was interesting seeing the look on Krispin's face when he came in and saw Trevor forcing himself upon me."

"What did you do? What did he do?"

"Krispin was the perfect gentleman. But he would have decked Trevor if I'd asked him to. I would have decked Trevor if Krispin hadn't come in. I was savage. That is, I was until I saw Krispin. Mom, isn't it kind of weird the Lord would use someone like Krispin to protect me?"

"It's weird, all right. But He used a donkey to speak to Baalam."

"True," Jess agreed, laughing. "Mom, tell Dad Krispin encrypted the co-op's computer as well as mine. He's some kind of expert in encryption."

"I'll let him know. And Jess, we'll be over sometime tonight. I won't guarantee it will be at nine."

Jess smiled. "Thanks. I appreciate it."

"You're welcome. Be careful, sweetheart."

"I will. I promise." Jess hung up the phone, grateful for the relationship with her stepmom. Dena had been the one to get Jess to see Trevor's faults and the problems with their relationship.

With the potatoes rinsed and in the oven, she flipped the steaks in the marinade and then started on the salad. She opted for a spinach and purple cabbage salad with a honey-mayo dressing. It was simple and easy to make. She'd only started learning how to cook since Dena had married her dad. She'd never had an interest in cooking before then. Instead, she used to pride herself on knowing all the delivery numbers in town.

Krispin pushed his dish away. "That was wonderful, Jess. I can't believe I've had two home-cooked meals in one day."

"Two? What was your first?"

"Greg Steadman and his wife had me over for lunch."

"They're a lovely couple."

"Yeah, and they've got a great bunch of kids."

"Do you like children?"

"Well enough. Truthfully, I hadn't given having children much thought." *Could I be a father one day? Would the Lord allow such a thing? That would be a huge blessing.*

"Randi having her baby has made me start to consider it. When Trevor and I were together, we thought eventually, one day. But neither one of us was in a hurry to have children. Of course back then I was going to run a Fortune 500 company in ten years, according to my plans."

"What changed?"

"The job. I discovered a certain amount of self-centeredness goes hand in hand with that kind of work. At least in the company I was working for. To be successful, you surrendered to the company at the expense of your life, and your personal goals were to get ahead at the expense of those around you. I guess if I had stayed in it, I would have found a way to work within the system, but after someone stole my idea and ran with it, it kind of let the wind out of my sails. Even when I could prove it was my proposal, the boss didn't care. He rewarded the thief. Can you believe that?"

"Yes, unfortunately. Let me guess, he was considered innovative."

"Yeah."

"Temp's dropping," he observed, changing the subject.

Jess looked away.

"I wasn't suggesting we go inside. I should be going."

"Krispin, no, I'm sorry. You've been the perfect gentleman, but—"

"But the first impression I gave you of myself still has you on pins and needles. Not a problem, Jess. I'm amazed that you even want to be alone with me."

"God's grace," Jess mumbled.

"I understand." Krispin stood up. "I'd offer to help with the dishes, but I think in this situation, it's best if I just leave."

"Krispin, thanks for all your help today. I don't know what I would have done without it."

Lost your identity or worse. "Not a problem. Again, thank you for such a wonderful dinner. I'll return the favor some-time, after I learn how to cook."

"Try the Food Network. It's been a huge help to me."

Krispin chuckled. "I'll try that. Good night, Jess."

"Night, Krispin."

He got to his car just as her parents drove up behind him in the driveway in the same Mercedes he'd seen Jess driving right after the accident.

"Hello, Mr. Black." Wayne extended his hand.

"This town's gossip line is something," Krispin grumbled as he accepted the proffered hand.

Wayne pulled him closer. "Actually, Jess asked us to swing by as a precaution."

Krispin felt the heat rise in his cheeks again. *So Jess doesn't trust me. I can't blame her, Lord.*

"I was just leaving." Krispin slipped behind the wheel of his car.

"Krispin," Dena Russell said as she came up beside his window. "We brought a game. Why don't you stay?"

Krispin's jaw tightened, then relaxed. He'd done everything in his power to have these people not trust him. Why was he overreacting? *Because you know you've changed, but they don't.* "Mrs. Russell, I really appreciate the offer, but I need to get home. I've been out all day."

Dena stepped back. "Maybe another time."

"That would be nice. Good night." He saw Jess give a weak

wave from the front porch. He knew he shouldn't be upset. But he couldn't help it. His past would keep him from having a future. He'd known it all along. Tonight he'd come face-to-face with that truth. He might be redeemed and certain God had forgiven him, but Jessica Kearns could never truly trust him.

ten

Jess felt bad for having invited her parents to come over—not because it wasn't the right thing to do, but because she hadn't told Krispin she'd invited them. The next few days passed with little or no contact from him. His new encryption software seemed to be working well. She still didn't like typing in twenty-five digits as her password, but then again, it was worth it.

Today, however, she was determined to make things right between them. Jess marched over to Krispin's workshop and reached for the old steel handle before noticing the brass padlock. Locked. She scanned the area for his car. Nothing. She headed back to the co-op and went to work, wondering how she could reconcile this situation.

Five hours later, she saw him drive through town with his car loaded with bags of groceries. Jess smiled.

She dialed his cell phone. "Where have you been shopping?"

Krispin chuckled. "You see me drive past?"

"Yupper. What's going on? Is there a huge sale at the store that I don't know about?"

"Nope, I went to Ellsworth and did some shopping after watching two days of the Food Network."

"You don't believe in doing things slowly, gradually working up to them, do you?"

"Guilty, I'm afraid."

Jess chuckled.

"Jess, would you like to come over and help me? I'm planning on cooking several meals ahead of time. Plus, I've got this new recipe for bruschetta that looks absolutely marvelous and a snap to make. What do you say?"

"Uh. . ." She paused.

"Jess? I'm not mad about the other night. After I had time to think about it, I understand why you called your folks. I would have appreciated a heads-up, but I understand. Look, I have enough food here to invite your parents to dinner, as well. What do you say?"

"Sure. Do you have all the pots, pans, and utensils you need?"

"I think so. I purchased a bunch of those, too."

"You're unbelievable."

"I believe in getting the proper tools for the job, even if I don't know how to use them yet. So when can you get here?"

"A half hour."

"Great, call your folks and invite them. Tell 'em I have no idea what's on the menu yet."

Jess laughed. "They'll love that."

"Good. See you soon."

By the time Jess arrived at Krispin's, he had taken all of the bags out of his car. Jess shut his open trunk as she headed to his back door. She knocked.

Krispin opened the door with his right hand, holding a bunch of green grapes in the other. "Hi, come on in."

"Have you ever frozen those whole?"

"No, why?"

"They're really good frozen in the hot summer. Very refreshing." Jess chuckled. "I was in college before Dad confessed that it also made them last longer 'cause I didn't sneak as many."

Krispin laughed along with her. "I'll have to freeze some. How do you do it? Pack them in a baggie?"

"Not at first. You place them on a cookie sheet, freeze them, then put them in a plastic bag or some other container. They're really good in sparkling cider, as well."

Krispin smiled and handed her the grapes. "Okay, you're on grape detail. Freeze half. The rest I need for the chicken salad and to munch on, of course."

Jess took the grapes. "Do you have a colander?"

"The strainer thingy?"

"Yup."

"In the living room in one of the bags on the sofa."

Jess walked over to the couch and found it littered with all kinds of kitchen equipment. "Wow, you've bought some really nice stuff. Just how much money did you make when you sold your share of the company?"

"Enough, but I purchased this with other money. I deposited that settlement check in a high-yield account for a couple months while I decide just how I'm going to invest it. Most of it I'll put aside for retirement so I won't have to pay taxes on it. I honestly don't know what I'm going to do yet, so I'd rather leave it untouched and in reserve until I have a definite direction."

"Why'd you leave your business? Why not a leave of absence?" Jess fished through the bags and pulled out the colander, then went to the sink and washed it.

"I burned out. I went five years without a vacation. Often I didn't even take the weekend off. I worked all the time."

"I kinda felt that way after college. I didn't want to see another book or take another test or write another paper for the rest of my life. A year later, I'm working on articles of incorporation and writing articles about why we should band together and sell our lobsters through a co-op."

"College was a snap compared to the last seven years. The first three years after school, work was easy. I went to work, did my job, got really good at what I did, and began the promotion process. Gary and I started to consult more often. He kept raising my position within the company, and then last year, something I'd done as a backup to my encryption program saved the company from a huge lawsuit and at the same time put us in the media spotlight. The flip side of that was I had every hacker in the world trying to break my codes.

I was working nonstop trying to stay one step ahead of the hackers. It was a horrible year for me." Krispin pulled out a cutting board and retrieved a new set of knives from the sofa. "Should I wash these?"

"Always. Anything you buy from the store for food prep should be washed before you use it. You don't know who might have sneezed on it in the store."

"Now that's gross." Krispin held the package by the tips of his fingers and carried it over to the sink.

"Those are nice knives."

"The set that comes with the cottage are horrible. I couldn't slice a tomato without squishing it."

"What are you making? And I'm done with the grapes. What do you want me to do next?"

"Okay, I'm going to make this bruschetta recipe. Would you take those boneless chicken breasts and bread them?" He turned around and fished out a container of preseasoned bread crumbs. "In the drawer under the oven, you'll find a baking dish you can use."

"All right."

"Are your folks coming?"

Jess laughed. "Yes, but they're a bit surprised."

"Did you explain to them it's going to be a wild night of experimental dishes?"

"I think that's what surprised them the most."

"I figure we can bring Jordan and Randi a couple of meals after we're done. After I make the bruschetta, I want to marinate the steaks. Oh, the recipe for the chicken with the bruschetta is on the counter. I bought a grill. We'll need to assemble it though. I thought we could make shish kebabs."

Jess continued to laugh. "I've never met anyone like you."

"Thanks, I think."

"Let me call Dad and tell him to bring his toolbox, or did you buy the wrench and screwdrivers to put the grill together?"

"Ah, I didn't buy those." Krispin hesitated. "I do have some at the shop. What kind do I need?"

"Don't bother. Dad will bring his."

"If you say so." Krispin started cutting the small grape tomatoes into tiny pieces. "What kind of potato or rice should we make for supper?"

"What are we having: the steak, chicken, or the shish kebabs?"

"All three?"

"Rice for the shish kebabs, baked potatoes for the steak."

"Okay, how do we bake potatoes?"

"You're serious, aren't you?"

"Yeah. They didn't cover making those on TV."

"Three-fifty for an hour in the oven."

They continued working on all kinds of food and various meals for the next thirty minutes. When her parents arrived, they were put right to work. By the end of the evening, they had made stuffed mushrooms, chicken bruschetta, shish kebabs, twice-baked potatoes, wild rice, corn on the cob, a tossed green salad, and had a roast cooking in the oven for roast beef sandwiches.

Krispin set aside two plates for Randi and Jordan. He also learned that his refrigerator wasn't big enough for all the food he'd purchased. Some went home with Jess, and some of the meat went home with her parents to put in their freezer.

She reflected on the wonderful evening, thinking about how she had never enjoyed cooking so much. Tonight she had seen in Krispin a passion for life that she'd never seen in him before. She liked it. His enthusiasm was contagious. She found herself still grinning when she settled between the covers to go to sleep in her own home. *Lord, he's amazing. I pray I'm being a good witness for You. Father, please help him find You. I think he's searching, Lord. I think he's even curious about You. He seemed to hang on every word Dad spoke when he was talking about the joy in knowing You. Please, Father, bring him to You.*

Krispin blew off the sawdust, then stood up tall and stretched his back. A reflexive moan followed. He never knew working at a counter for several hours would so strain the lower back. Of course he'd been discovering all kinds of muscles since moving to Squabbin Bay. Woodworking took one set; cooking took another. He'd had a blast with Jess and her parents last night. He couldn't wait until they could do it again. But every time he had looked over at Jess, his stomach did a flip. He needed to take this friendship very slowly.

"Hey, Krispin." Bryan, Greg's son, came running through the shop door. "Is it okay if I work with you and Daddy today?"

"Sure."

He ran out the door as fast as he'd come in through it. "Daddy, Krispin says it's okay."

Greg walked through the door with the boy in his arms. "Are you sure, Krispin? You mentioned at the house he could come, and he's been bothering me every day."

Krispin chuckled. "No problem."

"Great." Greg lowered the boy to the floor. "Go get your wood and tools, Bryan."

The boy scurried off again.

Greg walked over to the worktable where Krispin had laid out the Purpleheart strips. It was one of the more costly woods, but he felt the purple color would make great accent lines on the kayak.

"I love that wood," Greg said.

"Yeah, I'm really glad I decided to purchase the couple of boards."

"Would you like me to start sanding the yellow or red cedar strips?"

"Red, then the yellow. Thanks. That would be helpful."

Bryan came waddling in with his arms full of wood scraps. "Whatcha making, Bryan?"

"Daddy says we ain't got no money for expensive Christmas presents—"

"Bryan!" Greg scolded.

"Sorry, Daddy. I'm making Mommy a box to put things in."

"That sounds like a wonderful present."

"If I build it here, Mommy won't know, and Daddy says we have four months before Christmas. Course, once school starts, I can't do much buildin'."

Krispin held back a grin. Then he thought about Bryan's statement. Just how tight were the Steadmans? "Greg, I can pay you for helping me work on the kayaks."

"No, no, we're fine. We're always tight just before the season starts. Truth is, Bryan likes building things, and I felt it would be a good idea for him to make some presents this year."

"Understood. But I know I'm not going to use as much wood as I bought since you've been helping me out. So why don't you build yourself a kayak, too? I have more than enough wood."

Greg stroked his beard. "A canoe might be better for me and the family."

"Great, you make whatever you'd like. I'm sure we have plenty of wood for the two of us."

"You're certain? I wouldn't want to take the wood from you."

"Trust me, I'm certain. I don't think I could make another in the three months I have left in Squabbin Bay."

"Where ya going in three months?"

"I don't know."

"Daddy, can I help you build the canoe?"

"That would be up to Mr. Black."

Bryan pleaded with puppy dog eyes. "If you're well behaved, I don't have a problem, but you have to mind your father and me. There are some dangerous tools here."

"I will, I promise."

"All right."

For the next couple hours, the three of them worked hard. By lunchtime Bryan had reached his max. "I'll take him home. Krispin, are you sure about the wood?" Greg asked.

"Absolutely. And by the looks of it, I have more than enough fiberglass material, as well."

Greg extended his hand. "Thanks, Krispin. That's mighty generous of you."

"You're welcome. I can't tell you how much I appreciate your help and friendship."

Greg nodded. He scooped his worn-out son in his arms and carried him out the door. "I'll see you tomorrow."

Krispin looked at all the strips of sanded wood and all that remained to be sanded. He didn't think he'd make another one of these again, but he was glad for the experience. He was learning all kinds of new things. More importantly, Greg used the process to show him how God continued to sand off a person's rough edges. For the first time in Krispin's life, he was glad he wasn't God and in control. On the floor lay a broken and rough-cut piece of wood. *That was me a few months ago.* On the table were some pieces that had gone through the planer, nicely cut and semirefined. But they were nothing compared to the very smooth pieces that he and Greg had already sanded. The odd thing was that they would be sanded again and again before the kayak was finished. "Lord, you've got quite a project on your hands with me."

"Krispin?" Wayne Kearns called from behind the closed door.

eleven

Jess strained over the side of the boat to try and get a glimpse of what her father was doing in Krispin's shop. It was the second day in a row she had seen him enter the shop in the early afternoon. Truthfully, she had no reason to be on her boat, except to try and get a bird's-eye view into the shop's harbor doorway. He had to be helping Krispin with his kayak, she figured. Something, in all honesty, she'd love to be working on with him. The memories of making her kayak with her dad so many years ago flooded back every time she thought of Krispin making his.

For two days she'd been trying to come up with an excuse to get together with Krispin again but had come up with nothing. Jess turned from the starboard side of the boat and headed to the dock. She went back to the co-op and continued to work on next spring's advertising campaign.

Other small lobster fishermen were starting to contact the co-op to talk about joining the group. She'd had two inquiries so far this week. If the co-op continued growing at this rate, she'd have to start working full-time. The question was, when would the co-op be able to pay her salary? The balance between donated time and salary needs were quickly becoming a matter of discussion for the board of directors. And even then, she wasn't sure if she could handle everything in the office by herself much longer. She knew she could use a secretary or an administrative assistant, but the income didn't warrant it.

Jess scanned the preliminary ad campaign. It seemed flat, unengaging. Jess tapped the desk with her pen. "What's missing?"

"Me." Trevor stood in the doorway, beaming.

"Not!" Jess shook off her startled expression. "What are you doing here? What's going on, Trevor? When we broke up, I didn't hear from you. It's been well over a year now. What gives? When we were dating, I couldn't get you to come up for a visit, and here you are twice in a matter of a week or two."

"Now, Jess, hang on. Before I returned to the city, I thought I'd take one more stab at getting back together with you."

"Why? Nothing's changed."

"I've changed."

"Really. Would you be willing to live in Squabbin Bay?"

Trevor took a tentative step toward her desk. Jess stood up and held out her hands. "You stay right there, Trev."

"What's going on, Jess? You never were afraid of me before. I've got a job."

"Where? Doing what?"

"I'm a traveling salesman. Would you like to buy some knives?"

"No. Trev, I'm glad you've got a job. I'm glad it's working for you. My not living in the city was not the only thing wrong with our relationship. And you not wanting to get a job was another, but not the only reason, although that was major."

Trevor stepped back toward the door. "I think I've heard this conversation before. On that note, I'll take my leave. Tell me this, Jess. Are you happy?"

"Yeah, I am."

"I'm glad. Don't hate me too much, Jess. We had some good times."

Jess's spine relaxed. "Yeah, we did. Good luck with your job, Trev."

"Thanks. Hey, here's my business card if you ever decide you might like to buy some of these knives. They're pretty pricey. But they're excellent quality, with a lifetime guarantee." Trevor pulled a card out of his pocket.

Jess walked over and took it. "I'll keep it in mind."

Trevor turned the knob and opened the door. Looking back at her, he asked, "So are you dating the bodyguard?"

"Huh?"

"The guy that wanted to knock me into next week the last time I was here."

"Krispin? No."

"Ah, just curious. I'm sorry I blew it before, Jess. I hope you find the right person someday."

I do, too. "Same for you, Trev."

Trevor nodded his head and left. She had loved him once. He had seemed like the perfect Christian gentleman to blend with her. But she'd changed during college, too. It took graduating, having trouble getting the right job out of school, and then getting the dream job to show her the emptiness of that life she was headed for. It took coming home and getting grounded once again to show her who she really was in Christ. In the end she wouldn't have been happy married to Trevor. They looked at life and family in very different ways.

She thought about Krispin and what he had shared the other night about his life, his career, the emptiness of it all. *Dear Lord, thanks for saving me from that life. I could have gotten caught up in work and left You behind. Father, help me keep You central, even with the demands of the co-op pressing in on me.*

❧

Krispin scanned the shop. It had grown in use. Greg and his son Bryan were hard at work on their canoe. Wayne Kearns was spending a huge part of the day working on numerous projects since Dena had gone on a photo shoot for a few days. And Krispin had his kayak starting to take shape in his corner of the room. Krispin had also given Greg and Wayne their own keys to the shop.

But Krispin wanted to go home and work on the newest recipe he'd decided to make from watching television.

Cooking, for some odd reason, was really appealing to him, more than he'd ever thought possible. "Wayne, I'm going to put some shrimp and steak on the grill tonight. Would you like to join me?"

"I'd love to, but I'm having dinner with my folks before they return to Florida."

"How much longer will they be here?" Greg asked.

"Labor Day weekend. After that, they'll fly back to Florida. It's been a good visit."

"Glad to hear it."

Krispin knew the basic story from Jess. Greg had filled him in on some of the details regarding the townsfolk dropping as many charges as they could if Wayne's father got help for his gambling problem. It seemed odd, at first, to hear how the town would pull together behind an individual who had hurt so many. But what surprised him the most was that Wayne had sold his house and paid off all his father's debts, including what had been stolen from the lobstermen in terms of lost revenue. He was broke when he married Dena. Dena, who drove a Mercedes. Krispin wondered if he'd ever have the kind of love and forgiveness that Wayne and his family had demonstrated toward his father. It was so different from the world he'd been living in for the past ten years.

"Penny for your thoughts?" Wayne asked.

"Sorry, just thinking about my past, how I approached life."

"A lot to think about?"

"Yeah. I don't think I'll ever be as forgiving as you."

Wayne let out a nervous chuckle. "Let's hope you never have to."

Krispin paused. Didn't the Bible talk about God's grace being sufficient for whatever trials we encounter? *Where will I go and what am I going to do with myself after my six months are up?* "Wayne, my lease is up in November. Would you be interested in taking it over?"

Wayne rubbed the back of his neck with a handkerchief.

"Let me think on that. A shop to work on some cabinets would be nice. We don't really have the room at the house. What's the rent?"

They discussed the lease arrangements Krispin had made with the owner, then went back to work. Greg and Bryan left first. Krispin put away his tools and cleaned up the shop, except around where Wayne was still working. "I'll lock up," Wayne offered.

"Thanks." Krispin left. The cool, crisp air of early fall invigorated him. A thought to invite Jess for dinner breezed through his mind. He sat down in his car and tapped the steering wheel, debating whether or not he should invite Jess to dinner tonight. Deciding to throw caution to the wind, he placed a call on his cell and turned the key.

"Jess, it's Krispin."

"Hey, what's up?"

"Dinner, my place, steak and shrimp on the grill. What do you say?" He glanced in the rearview mirror before putting the car in reverse.

"I'd love to, but I can't. Sorry."

They said their good-byes, and he dialed Randi and Jordan's only to find that they were busy, too. He passed a roadside stand and grabbed a couple of ears of corn. He'd throw the second steak in the freezer and eat the shrimp instead.

His phone rang as he drove up the scalloped-shell drive-way. "Hello."

"Krispin, it's me, Jess. There's a problem with my home computer. I have dinner plans with Dad and my grandparents tonight. Can you come by and fix it while I'm out?"

"Sure, what's it doing?"

"It won't turn on."

Fear sliced through his backbone. Someone had tried to retrieve the Trojan horse program he had found on her computer. "All right. Where will you leave a key?"

"I'll drop it off on my way out to my parents' house."

"Okay, see you in a few."

"Great, thanks."

He clicked his phone shut and debated whether or not he should have told Jess that someone probably tried to break into the computer. Not wanting to worry her, he decided to keep that to himself until he knew for sure.

Krispin grabbed the corn and headed to the kitchen. *Should I warn her, Lord? What if the intruder is in the house? Is she in danger?*

He dialed Jess's house. It rang. . .no answer. He paced back and forth in his kitchen. It rang a second time. . .still no answer. "Pick up, Jess." Third ring, again no answer. "Come on, Jess." Fourth ring. He hung up and called the sheriff.

"Sheriff McKean, it's Krispin Black. I'm concerned about Jessica Kearns. I just called her house and there was no answer."

"Now, son, just because she's not—"

"Sorry, she just called me, said her computer wouldn't start up. I put a safety in the computer program I installed that has the computer look like it won't turn on if an unauthorized person tried to access her computer." He didn't have time to explain everything. "Look, what if whoever broke into the computer is in the house? Couldn't she be in—"

"I'm on my way. You sit tight."

Krispin hung up the phone. Unable from the time he was thirteen to just sit tight when his elders told him to, Krispin got into his car and drove over to Jess's. As he turned into her drive, he saw the sheriff's car parked beside hers. The sheriff stood outside the back door, talking with Jess. Her hair was wrapped in a towel, and she was dressed in a terry robe she held tightly across her chest. She glanced over at him and frowned.

Oh boy. He responded with a wave.

Jess turned back into the house. The sheriff approached him.

"You don't listen well, do you?"

"Sorry. Shower?"

"Ayup. Look, Krispin, I don't mean to be telling you your business, but you should have told Jess what could have happened with her computer."

"I didn't want to alarm her."

"Instead you alarmed me and had me come over and roust her out of a shower."

"Right. I'm sorry."

The sheriff tapped the upper part of the door. "She told me to tell you to wait and she'd hand you the keys." He walked toward his car.

"Thanks, Sheriff." Krispin's mind swirled. How could he make things right with Jess? *You could start by telling her you believe in Me.*

His body went rigid. Had God just spoken to him?

He placed a call to Pastor Russell.

"Hello?" Marie, the pastor's wife, answered.

"Hi, Marie, it's Krispin Black. Is Pastor Russell free?"

"Sure, let me get him."

Krispin tapped the steering wheel, waiting for the pastor.

"Hi, Krispin. What can I do for you?"

"Pastor Russell, I'm wondering if you ever hear God's voice." *How do I explain this?* "It was like a voice in my head."

"Yes, I've had that experience. The caution is to test what the voice says and make sure it's not telling you something contrary to the Bible."

From everything Krispin had read in the Bible so far, this wasn't contrary. In fact, several places in it said to tell others that you believe in God. "Okay, thanks."

"Is that it?"

Krispin chuckled. "Yeah. Pretty dumb question, huh?"

"No, actually there are many who never 'hear' a distinct voice from God. Pray and seek the Lord, Krispin. You're doing well."

"Thanks."

Jess opened the back door.

"I've got to go, Pastor. See you Sunday."

"Bye." Pastor Russell hung up.

Krispin started to shake. He wanted to tell Jess, but he'd also wanted her to see the changes in him and recognize what had taken place in his life for herself.

"Krispin, why didn't you tell me about the program?"

"Sorry. I didn't want to scare you."

Jess leaned in toward him. "I'm not a child that needs to be protected."

"I'm sorry, Jess. I didn't mean to offend you. If you remember, I had to run off after I installed the security program. I simply forgot to mention it. I can fix it, but it does mean that someone probably came into your house."

"I understand, and the sheriff checked the exterior before you arrived. Krispin, it isn't your job to protect me."

But I want to. "I know. I'm sorry. It won't happen again."

She leaned back on her heels and handed him the keys. "I've got to go. I'm going to be late as it is. Call me if you find anything on the computer."

"I will."

Jess left his side and slipped behind the wheel of her car. The cold metal of the keys felt like the coldness around his heart. Jess didn't love him, at least not like he loved her. He went inside, sat down at her computer, reset the security program, and left in a span of fifteen minutes.

Back at home, his appetite faded. He put a sandwich together and saved the steak and shrimp for another time. Tomorrow he'd have to tell Jess the full truth of why he had come back to Squabbin Bay and that he was now a Christian.

twelve

The brisk early morning air lapped Jess's cheeks as she walked to her car. The only noise was the swooshing of her foul-weather gear sounding like a huge, thick pair of rubber gloves walking down the street. They made their final *squeak* as she sat down behind the wheel of her car and drove to the harbor. Walking down the steep incline of the dock due to low tide, she held on to the rail. She glanced over to the spot where she had run over Krispin and his kayak.

She closed her eyes and paused for a moment, saying another prayer for him, then added, *Lord, help me forgive myself for not seeing him that day.* For the past two weeks, she'd been avoiding him.

The shadow of a man's profile stood on the deck of her boat. The muscles on the back of her neck tightened. "Hello?"

"It's me, Jess."

"Krispin?" Jess relaxed.

"Yes. We need to talk."

She came toward him. "What are you doing here?"

"You've been avoiding me. I decided to take matters into my own hands and came where I knew you would be." He rubbed his arms.

"Are you cold?"

"A little. There's a lot of moisture in the air."

"How long have you been here?"

"An hour. I wasn't sure when you would arrive, so I came early." He took a step toward her. "Jess, I'm sorry about the computer program, calling the sheriff."

Jess snickered. "Krispin, that's not the problem."

He paused for a moment. "May I go out with you this

morning so we can talk?"

Did she want to be alone with him, really alone? "You can trust me, Jess."

"All right. But you'll need some foul-weather gear. It's too cold without it. Let me get Dad's from the shed." She went over to the small shack standing on the end of the dock that abutted the granite cliff walls lining the harbor and reached for her dad's yellow, foul-weather gear. Her gear was orange. She'd chosen the different color to stand out from others.

"Thanks."

"Just slip them on over your clothing. I'm afraid Dad's boots won't fit you, though."

"That's all right. These will help."

"You get dressed. I need to make the boat ready." Returning to the shed, she grabbed the chum buckets and set them on the edge of the dock. She gathered some extra nets for the pots in case she found any that had been destroyed.

Krispin loaded the chum buckets on deck. "These stink."

Jess laughed. "You haven't smelled anything yet." Grabbing a couple more chum bags, she headed back to the boat.

The engines came to life with a roar at the twist of a key. She set it in neutral and started to cast off.

"Can I help?"

"No, thanks. I have this down so I can pretty much do it in my sleep."

"Ah." Krispin turned and sat down on the bench on the port side of the boat.

Stepping back on board, Jess got behind the wheel and shifted the lever into reverse. Slowly the boat pulled away from the dock. She circled around in reverse, then pushed the throttle into forward and headed out of the harbor. The gentle ribbon of first light shone on the eastern horizon.

"Do you get up this early every morning?"

"Only on Tuesdays. The co-op needs a lot of my attention on Tuesdays."

"How is the co-op doing? Any more attempts to access your computers?"

"No. And thank you for fixing them."

"You're welcome." He stood on the deck and came up beside her. "Jess, I don't know what I did, but I'm sorry."

"Krispin." She paused. It was time to confess. He needed to understand why she couldn't see him anymore. "It's not you, it's me."

"No, it's me. I know how rude I was to you the day you saved my life."

"It's not that, Krispin."

"No, I suppose it isn't. Look, before you say anything, I need to tell you something. I've been fighting it for a long time, but if I don't tell you soon, I'm going to explode. Well, I don't think I'll explode exactly."

"You're rambling."

"Right, sorry. Okay, here's the deal. I came back to Squabbin Bay to find God."

"What?"

He took in a deep breath and let it out slowly. "Your father challenged me the day I left. Life had gotten very boring and complicated. I wasn't satisfied by what I'd earned, done, or even who I was anymore. I didn't enjoy the competitiveness of my industry any longer, and I knew my company would suffer if I wasn't driven the way I had been before. Anyway, all of that is to say that the accident and what your father said made me reevaluate my life—where I was headed and why I was here. I didn't tell you because of what you said to me before."

"What?"

"That you wouldn't get involved with a man who didn't believe like you did. I didn't want you to think I became a Christian so I could date you."

Jess started to giggle. "Does my father know?"

"Yeah, sorry. I asked him not to say anything. I wanted you

to see a change in me, not have me tell you. But ever since that night when someone tried to access your computer, I've known I was supposed to tell you. In fact, I was going to tell you the next morning, but I couldn't find you. Then it just got easier and easier to avoid you because you were avoiding me. But it really hasn't been all that easy. I keep being encouraged by the Lord to tell you. I couldn't resist any longer, and that's why I staked out your boat."

Jess clenched the steering wheel, aiming for the red light that marked the port side entrance to the harbor. "You're truly saved?"

"Yeah, sinner that I am."

"So that's why you've been visiting with my stepbrother? And Greg Steadman?"

"He's my mentor."

"Unbelievable."

"What? Why? Can't a guy like me get saved?"

Jess relaxed. "No, it isn't that. What's unbelievable is what I was going to confess to you."

"Shoot."

"Krispin, I had to tell you I couldn't see you anymore because. . ." Should she confess it? *But if he's saved, what's the problem?*

"Because you're attracted to me?"

"Right," she admitted.

"I avoided you for that very reason. And I'm still not sure that you and I should see a lot of each other. I still have a long ways to grow as a Christian. I'm not sure we should get too involved at this point in time."

Jess looked at the compass. It was her only navigator at this time of day. She set out on her heading, glanced at the clock, and worked her way down the western shoreline. She had to concentrate on where she was going. If she gave in to her emotions, she'd get distracted by their conversation and lose her bearings, and they'd be out far longer than they should be.

"Jess?"

"Sorry. I'm not sure what to say. I think we need to get to know one another better."

"I agree. Being friends is a good place to start." The wind and chop of the water grew with intensity as they left the confines of the harbor. The hull bounced hard on the water. Jess steadied her sea legs and positioned for the impact.

Krispin slipped and grabbed the helm, keeping himself from falling.

"Sorry. I should have warned you."

"No problem. Look, I'm not just attracted to you. Wait, that didn't come out right. Hang on." He paused. Jess held back a grin. She knew exactly what he was thinking, but it was too soon. Too soon for them to consider a life with one another and too soon for him as a new Christian to consider marriage.

"I'm not saying this right, but here it goes. I'm not just physically attracted to you. I'm attracted to you as a person— who you are, how you do things, the way you smile. The way you look at life. The way you treated me after I was so horribly rude to you. All of that and so much more. I even love the way you gently nibble your upper lip when you're concentrating on something."

"I do what?"

"You roll your upper lip slightly and press your lower lip against it, like so."

She watched him do the very thing he just described. "I do not."

Krispin chuckled. "Yes, you do. I've seen you. I'll point it out next time."

"Well, you have a few personality traits of your own, you know."

"Oh really? Like what?"

The horizon was brightening behind them. "For example, you rub the back of your neck when you're not sure what to say or do."

Krispin pulled his hand down from the back of his neck.

"All right, I'll give you that one."

They bounced along with the waves for a couple of minutes, neither knowing what to say next. *To admit I'm attracted to him before I really get to know him. . .* Jess shook off the thought. "What are you going to do with yourself once you leave Squabbin Bay?"

"I don't know. One thing is certain, I won't be going into boat building. Greg and his son's canoe is farther along than mine, and I had a two-month head start."

"I enjoyed building mine with my dad, but only because I was building it with Dad. I do have a few skills that have helped me repair a thing or two around the house, though. I'm certain I wouldn't have known what to do if I hadn't built that kayak with Dad."

"And I'm learning how to use power tools. Never used any before, not even in shop. The school budget was cut that year so all the guys who signed up for shop got to take an extra music or gym class. Or we could have taken home ec, but that was a sissy class in my neck of the woods."

"Where'd you grow up?"

"Outside of Manchester, a small town called South Hooksett. The sun's coming up."

"Yeah, by the time I reach the first pot, the sun is cresting the horizon. See that bluff?" She pointed to the largest bluff jutting out from the shore farther up. "That's Mom and Dad's place."

"Nice location."

"Yeah. Dena rented it from the previous owner, but when he decided to put it on the market, she bought it and had Dad put the addition on. One thing led to another and boom—they got married."

"You seem happy with your stepmother."

"Very. She's the mother I never had. I visited with my bio-mom earlier this summer; it was the first time since Dena and Dad married. It was odd. I don't have any real connection to her. I mean, there are things in my temperament that I realize I got from her genes, but the most we'll ever have in common is an occasional friendship where we connect every now and again. I don't fit in her world. Truthfully, I never fit in her world at all."

"My folks are still married, but we're not very close. I love them, but they aren't the kind of people who make great friendships with others. They tend to be lost in themselves. Even when we were small children, they seemed to leave us behind and go off with one another. Eating meals together was done in silence. They never asked questions. I envy the relationship you have with your family. I'd never have known you weren't Dena's daughter by the way you all respond to one another."

"I had a great relationship with my dad. He spoiled me rotten. Fortunately, he worked hard for the little money he had or he would have gone overboard with expensive gifts I didn't need. Instead, he gave of himself by being the dad at every school event, going out with the Girl Scout troop events. Trust me, he was the only father at those events, except the father-daughter banquets. Scouting always brings out the mothers. Even Boy Scouts have den mothers. My dad was the first man, and probably the last, to attend such functions. And the girls were horrible to him. They'd giggle and tease him. He'd pitch his tent on the other side of the campground just to get some sleep at night. Anyway, Dad took me everywhere and did everything with me. When I was sixteen, I wished he'd go away. Thankfully he didn't, and I'm a better person because of it."

"I like your dad. He tells it like it is."

"Yeah." She slowed the engine and shifted it to neutral. "Here we go."

"What can I do?"

"Nothing, just watch."

"Okay." He crossed his arms and stood with his legs apart. Jess smiled. He'd gotten a handle on his sea legs.

"Seriously, watch me so you can see what I'm doing."

"Okay."

She fished the buoy out. "First, I hook the rope with this gaff hook. Then I place the line into this pulley. With the push of a button, it reels in the pot. I had Dad buy these, and I love them. I don't have to haul up each pot by hand."

The winch hummed, and the rope spooled up. "From this point"—the pot hung above the water—"I pull the pot over here and slide it on this table, like so."

"How many pots do you have?"

"Only two hundred."

"But you've got six lobsters in there."

"Not all the pots will have lobsters. See this one?" She held a mother lobster upside down, her eggs fully coating her tail. "She goes back. Those black circles are eggs."

"Awesome."

"You haven't been around sea or country life much, have you?"

"Nope. We lived in South Hooksett, but my folks had us in Manchester schools. By the time I was ten, I was in a private school. Country life is something I know little about."

"All right. But this is country on the sea, and people who grow up on the shore are different than plain old country folk."

"Hmm, I have a lot to learn."

"You betcha. Now for the nasty part." Jess flipped open the bucket of chum.

"Gross! What is that?"

"Rotting fish."

"Double gross. What are you doing?"

"Lobsters are bottom feeders, scavengers. They eat what they can find on the bottom of the ocean. Generally, that's dead fish."

"Yuck. I knew I didn't care for lobster for a reason."

She laughed.

Jess reached her hand into the chum bucket, and Krispin leaned over the side of the boat and nearly lost his breakfast—no wait, supper. He hadn't eaten this morning. The smell was the most foul he'd ever encountered.

"The smellier, the better."

She placed the chum in a bag of what appeared to be cheese-cloth-type material and tied it down on a spike in front of the net where the lobsters were housed.

"You do this every day?"

"Just about."

"Man, how can you stand it?"

"You get used to it."

Not on your life. "Isn't there fake bait or something you could use?"

"Nope. Real stuff. You can't fool a lobster."

She lifted a panel in the center of the boat. Water lapped against the hull. "What's that? Are we sinking?"

"A holding tank. We sealed off a section of the boat hull and vented it to the ocean. The lobsters stay alive even if we can't unload them right away. Most don't do that, but one winter Dad and I had nothing better to do, so we made it out of fiberglass and wood."

Krispin eased in for a better look. He had to admit, he was still timid around the water. But for Jess, he'd do anything. Well, anything but touch that awful chum. Thankfully, she wore gloves. He shuddered just thinking about that smell.

"Once the pot is ready, we toss it back in and move on to the next one."

"You do this a couple hundred times?"

"No, only one hundred, then tomorrow the other half."

"I'm amazed. That's a lot of work for a little return."

"Maybe. But it is honest work, and unlike yourself, a lot of people like lobster."

"True. Supply and demand."

"Ayup," she said in her Down-Eastern accent. "You said you went into computer programming because you liked numbers."

"Yeah. Then as I got older, I found ways to make those numbers cash numbers. I liked that even better."

"Okay, wrap your head around this. If I catch an average of a 150 to 200 lobsters every day, that's 6 times a week, and each lobster pulled in an average of $12 a piece wholesale, how much can I earn in a year?" She paused. "Oh, and figure in for only 40 weeks."

"Okay. At 150 lobsters per day, six days a week, that's 900 a week and 36,000 a year. Earning $12 per lobster, that's $1,800 per day, for a grand total of $432,000 a year." He whistled. "I thought you were poor, relatively speaking."

"I said I didn't earn much. Here's the thing: We don't average that much per sale. For the bigger orders, we can get as little as $6 for a pound-and-a-half lobster. Some online businesses are selling their lobsters for a premium price, but they're buying them from the fisherman for a lot less. That's the reason I started the co-op: to try and get a better price for our product without going through the roof so that a typical lobster dinner doesn't cost what it costs in New York City."

"We'd order them from a caterer for our corporate parties. Lobster isn't cheap."

Jess continued to pull up pot after pot.

"Basically, you're saying you have a lot more earning potential than you're currently doing."

"Yes. But it's not only about the profit. It's also about making it a more steady income."

"Why only forty weeks?"

"We don't lobster in the really bad winter months. Even with foul-weather gear, you freeze out here. Commercial fishermen go all year, but they can be out on the sea for a month and bring in a hefty salary. But that isn't the kind of a life I want to live. Have you seen some of those programs about those dangerous jobs? Lobstering is one of them, for the commercial fishermen."

"I can imagine." Krispin was enjoying the warmth of the sun's rays as it came up over the horizon. Jess fascinated him. How could she do this day after day and still like it? "Jess, do you honestly enjoy doing this?"

Jess reached into the bucket and pulled out another brown, bloody, chunky handful of rotting fish. Krispin held on to his stomach. *Lord, help me get over that smell.*

"Yeah, it's crazy. I know. A woman who likes lobstering. I like being out on the water. Four years of college and little time on the ocean showed me how much I missed it. But when I moved to Boston and started working in the city, the commute wasn't quite as early as when I get up for lobstering, but it was early enough. Still dark in the morning when I'd leave, I'd smell diesel and road grime. Here I smell the ocean, feel the wind on my face, roll with the waves. . . . It's more peaceful."

"Yeah, but the smell?" Krispin held his nose and waved off the stench of decaying fish.

The lilt of Jess's laughter caused him to relax. "I know. I said the same to Dad, year after year. Trust me, Randi thinks it's odd, too.

"So," Jess continued, "tell me more about your newfound faith."

thirteen

"I'm still putting the pieces together," Krispin said. "I believe in God and that He has a perfect plan for me. Jesus and His need to come to earth and die for my sins is more real to me than it was the day I asked Him into my heart. But I'm still not sure of my purpose in this world. Before I found the Lord, my life wasn't adding up. I'd done all you were supposed to do, and then some, and still I wasn't satisfied. In programming that's a good thing, because you constantly have to rewrite and build new and more powerful components to the software. But for life, it left me feeling empty and alone. Truthfully, I don't feel that much different. There's a calmness inside me. No, it's more like a contentment, a sense of peace that everything will work out fine."

Jess watched as Krispin's face turned a light shade of green. "Are you all right?"

"I will be, I hope," he muttered.

"Okay, the key is to not think about it. The chum is simply what is needed to catch lobsters—the bait."

"I've never been one for fishing."

Jess fastened the bait bag around the spike in the center of the pot. "How do you feel about fishing for men?"

Krispin chuckled. "I'm getting more comfortable with the idea. I don't want to be one of those guys who tells everyone that they need to be saved. I mean, it's true they need to know Jesus and accept Him as their Savior, but—I don't know, I've never been the salesman type. I let others in the company do that. I was more involved with the day-to-day numbers and code to write the software."

"So what made Jesus real for you?" Jess closed the pot and

plopped it back in the water.

She went to the helm and switched gears; the boat's propellers churned the waters off the stern. "Hang on, we're heading back in. Come, sit up here next to me. You won't be as cold, and hopefully the smell will remain behind us."

Krispin navigated to the seat next to hers.

"So are you satisfied now?"

"I'm confused more than anything. I know I'll go back to work eventually. I'm too young to retire, and what I made off of the sale will hold me for a while but not the rest of my life. I liked work, just not the stress of the partnership. I'm the kind of guy you can lock in a room with a computer, and I'd be happy for days. But the past few years, I've dealt with the clients more, and I discovered I liked having a social life. A few years back, when nerds were cool, I suppose that's when I started changing from the quiet geek to the rude, crude, and socially unacceptable guy I was when you first met me."

Jess smiled. He didn't seem the same man at all. She couldn't put her finger on it, but he seemed almost depressed, and certainly not as confident as he had been. "Krispin, who is the real you? I mean, when you were a kid, what were you like around other children?"

"I never really had childhood friends. School was a snap for me. I was bored. So I read or worked on math problems. I was doing algebra by the fourth grade. You know, I've never really fit. At work I was popular because of what I offered the company. College was a bore. I didn't have to work hard to get the grades, so I started to party all the time, and that's back when geeks were popular with the girls." He paused for a moment.

The hull of the boat jumped and banged against the waves. Jess glanced back at the compass heading.

"Since I became a Christian, I don't seem to fit in anywhere again. I feel kind of like the young school boy in the private academy, in my room, enjoying my study, but not enjoying my life."

Jess reached over and placed her ungloved hand on his arm. "You need to start enjoying life."

"Yeah, but I. . .well, I feel so guilty. The things I found pleasure in before don't even interest me now."

"Ah, okay. Let's correct that. Why don't you meet me for an evening kayak ride in the harbor? You can use Dad's."

A slow smile eased up his handsome cheeks. *Lord, if this man is who you've planned for me, keep him around. If he's not, move him soon. I don't think my heart can take it.*

"All right. Can you come back to my place for dinner?"

Jess paused and wondered if she had the strength to visit and not give in to moving their relationship too quickly forward.

As if reading her mind, he offered, "You can invite your folks or anyone else to join us. I don't mind."

"No. It'll be all right. Let's just promise ourselves we won't move too quickly, too soon."

The small lines that ran across his forehead when he thought intently on things furrowed. Slowly he nodded his head. "Yes, let's keep each other accountable that way."

❧

Krispin feared he shouldn't have revealed so much of his confusion. *Father, go before us and help us. Help me determine what is right and holy in our relationship*, he prayed.

He still had many of the same questions he had before he asked Jesus to come into his life. The difference was he was content with not knowing. But he was a babe in the woods when it came to understanding how to relate to others on a personal level. It was one thing to be the handsome guy pursuing a new conquest, but to be an honorable man in pursuit of a wife. . .that was totally new to him. He'd avoided marriage in his former lifestyle and made his aversion to it clear to the women around him. Now, he still felt shame for his past. How could Jess ever love him with that hanging over him?

They were pulling back into the harbor. "Thanks, Jess. I'm glad I came out."

"Me, too."

"Can I lend you a hand once we get into port?" he asked, hoping the answer would be no if it came to that chum bucket. His stomach rolled just thinking about it.

Jess chuckled. "No, thanks. Dad will be around soon to lend me a hand. Then I've got to run home, clean up, and go to the office."

Jess slowed her approach. It seemed slower than the other fishermen. "Are you still having problems about running over me?"

Jess's knuckles whitened as she tightened her grip around the steering wheel.

"Jess, I was just as much at fault as you were. I wasn't looking and had been under the pier just before you hit me."

"What?"

"I had taken my kayak under the pier to get a look at some of the sea life living on the pilings. I pulled out without thinking. My mind was on work and the problems I was having with the company. I wasn't thinking about where I was or what I was doing. You couldn't have avoided me. I'm certain of it. I owe you my life, Jess."

"Then why. . ." Her words trailed off.

"The lawsuit?" he finished for her. "Because I was a cad."

Jess nodded.

One of those awkward moments passed between them, until the boat gently rubbed against the pilings. Krispin jumped up and took the stern line with him. He secured the rear line of the boat while Jess moved up to the bow. He took off the yellow foul-weather gear and laid it on the bench of their fishing shack. "I'll see you later, Jess."

Jess came up beside him. Her honey-wheat hair glistened in the morning light. Her blue eyes dazzled him. Krispin swallowed. He wanted to kiss her. He refused to act on such an impulse.

Placing her hand on his chest, she whispered, "Thanks for telling me that. I've had many a sleepless night trying to figure out how I—"

He reached out and pulled her close. "Jess, I'm so sorry. Please forgive me."

Jess nodded her head against his chest. "I do."

His heart wanted to burst. The woman he loved, the woman he'd been so incredibly rude to, was in his arms and forgiving him for the cad he had been. "Thank you for saving my life, Jess. My soul," he whispered.

Jess pulled away first. Krispin stepped back. "I'll see you later."

Jess smiled. "Later."

Krispin hiked up the walkway back to the street level of the harbor. He turned back to see Jess working. When she pulled the bucket of chum out of the boat, his stomach flipped once again. He needed a shower and a nap.

His cell phone rang. "Hello?"

"Hi, Krispin. Pastor Russell here."

"Hi, Pastor. What's up?"

"I was confirming that you would be giving your testimony in church tomorrow morning."

"Yes." *Another reason I had to tell Jess the truth—before she heard my public testimony.*

"Great. I'll see you later."

"Later?"

"I take it you've forgotten the meeting of the men and their mentors tonight? A barbecue at the church."

Krispin let out a nervous chuckle. "Afraid so. I'll be there."

"See you soon."

Krispin said good-bye and immediately called and left a message on Jess's answering machine that he had to cancel their evening plans. Although he definitely would prefer to be in Jess's company, perhaps it was wise that they not be alone together too often after declaring their attraction to one another.

Later that evening, he found himself pleasantly surprised, enjoying the company of the men around him. Wayne stood at the grill with Pastor Russell. Greg Steadman came up to him with a plate brimming with food and an inch-thick stack of napkins. "Now don't you tell my wife. She says I could stand to lose twenty pounds."

Krispin chuckled. "My lips are sealed."

"Good." Greg sat down beside him. "I saw you went out on the boat with Jess this morning. Are you two dating?"

"No," Krispin answered a bit defensively. "We're friends. But we're talking about the possibility, maybe bringing our relationship to the next level. Do you know she still feels guilty for running over me?"

"I suspect she will for a while." Greg picked up a rib and bit into it. Barbecue sauce stained the edges of his beard. Krispin now understood the large pile of napkins Greg had brought with him, as he automatically wiped his beard after every bite.

"I told her on the boat."

"Told her what?"

Krispin sighed. "That I am a Christian. I didn't want her to hear my testimony in church tomorrow without having heard it from me first."

"Makes sense. But what about her seeing you live a different lifestyle first?"

"I tried that, but for the past two weeks, she's been avoiding me. So I thought it best to get it out in the open once and for all."

"Krispin, you told me you didn't become a Christian to get the girl. Are you still sure?"

"Yeah, I'm sure. God is real, and I've noticed a change in my life. Although some of the changes aren't all that pleasant."

"Like?" Greg continued to eat.

"I had a strange childhood."

"You mentioned that. But what in particular is striking you now?"

Krispin paused, scanned the area, and noted that Wayne still stood by the grill. Krispin lowered his voice. "When I was a child, I never learned to socialize with the other children. I was a loner. I liked it. Or rather, I preferred it over being teased about being so smart. When I went off to boarding school, I didn't know anyone, and it basically stayed that way until college, when I discovered a certain popularity with the women.

"Anyway," Krispin went on, "fact is, I really don't know how to act around a woman that I'm not trying. . .well, you know."

"Are you trying to with Jess?"

"Oh no, never! I mean. . ." Krispin stumbled over his words. "I respect her too much. I would never try to. . .you know."

Greg smiled and nodded.

"Yeah, I know. When Jayne and I met, I had similar ideas. The thing to do is to pray about it. God will give you the wisdom, the control, and the understanding in how this will all work out."

"I wish He'd just tell me and get it over with," Krispin mumbled.

"You and just about every other Christian on the planet. That's what trust is all about."

"But if the Bible is right, I have way too many wives as it is now. How do I reconcile what I've done in the past with who I am now?"

"You're forgetting that forgiveness clause. All your sins— and I do mean *all* your sins—have been forgiven."

Another man was heading toward the table—Jim or John or something like that. Krispin couldn't remember. "Hello," he said. "Would you care to sit here?"

"Josiah, take a load off." Greg pointed to the chair beside

him. "Josiah, meet Krispin. Krispin, Josiah."

The two men shook hands. Krispin went back to his meal. "Josiah here has an incredible problem," Greg said. "He's about to go to prison."

"Sorry to hear that."

"I deserve it. I conned my grandfather out of his life savings. He has nothing left. The only downside is that I can't earn the money from prison to take care of him. My family won't speak to me; my wife left and returned to her parents. Last I heard, I was going to be a father in a month, but my wife isn't communicating with me."

"Ouch."

"Yeah. 'If you do the crime. . .'"

"You do the time," Pastor Russell said as he sat down beside Krispin. "You're turning yourself in tomorrow morning?"

"Yes. Today is my last day as a free man. However, the sheriff says I'll be coming to church with him in the morning 'cause he doesn't want to watch the cell, which means I can give my testimony before I go in."

"Wonderful. Tomorrow's service will be very different."

Krispin forked his coleslaw. He wondered what kind of a testimony Josiah had. He couldn't imagine stealing from someone, let alone from his own grandfather, and leaving him with nothing.

"Grandpa says he'll be here in the morning, too."

"Good," Pastor Russell answered without much of a reaction.

Krispin watched as Josiah ate his food. He seemed content going to jail and remorseful that he was leaving his grandfather in such scrapes. "What does your grandfather do?" Krispin asked.

"Lobstering, now. When he was a young man, he worked at the granite quarries."

How old is his grandfather? Krispin's thoughts flooded with memories of the early morning hours, the cool damp air, the weight of the lobster pots being pulled on board. *How can an old man do what Jess does?* he wondered.

"What about yourself, Krispin? Aren't you the man Jessica Kearns ran over with her boat?"

"Yes, but it wasn't only her fault. I should have paid more attention."

"More than likely. Most folks know well enough not to try and outrun a motorboat with a paddle." Josiah smiled. "Seriously, dude, what are you doing here? Didn't you threaten to sue Jess, her father, and the co-op?"

"Only Jess." Realizing he was being defensive, Krispin added, "I saw something in her and her father that made me curious about God."

"I wished I'd paid more attention when Mr. Kearns was my youth leader. I wouldn't have ruined so many lives. But enough about me. I've got the next five years to think about it. Word on the street is you're some kinda computer genius or something."

"I wrote software. I'm not a computer genius."

Greg smiled and placed his hand on Josiah. "Math is easy for him, like it is for my Lissa."

Josiah held a cob of corn in his hand and thought for a moment, then narrowed his hazel gaze on Krispin. "How do we know you're not the one that tried to break into Jess's computers?"

Krispin's spine stiffened, then he relaxed a fraction. "Frankly, you don't. But in my line of business, I have to be above reproach. I've been investigated more than once and have always stood the test. If I were not a man to be trusted, no one would buy our software. It's not just me that needs to trust in my abilities and honor. All of my clients have to trust me. And for what it's worth, I'm bonded." Krispin stood up. "Excuse me, I'm going to get some more corn."

He took a couple of steps, then turned back and leveled his gaze on Josiah. "To add to all the professional accolades,

I now have Jesus in my court. God knows it wasn't me, and He knows who it was. I don't have to worry anymore with Him on my side."

fourteen

Jess caught herself wiggling in the pew as she waited for the morning service to begin. *Face it, girl, you've been wound up tighter than a rope spun around the propeller.* All night she'd been thinking about Krispin's confession and wondering how she hadn't picked up on the change in him. She had noticed he no longer behaved like a Neanderthal and that he was actually a kind and considerate person. Like when he asked his friend to fly Jordan back to Squabbin Bay in time for him to be at Randi's side for the birth of their baby. She had seen how generous he'd been to Greg Steadman and his family and how helpful he'd been to her with her computer problems. All in all, he did not seem to be anything like the man she had pulled out of the harbor those many months ago.

A smile of pleasure crossed her lips. She couldn't wait to tell Krispin of her observations. Admittedly, she had been overly guarded on the boat, fearful that it was another manipulative ploy on his part. But throughout the day and night, more confirmations about Krispin's faith and actions became clearer, along with her own guilt for not really trusting him. *Forgive me, Lord.*

Jess glanced over to the front pew where Krispin and the others sat waiting to give their testimonies. Krispin's gaze locked with hers. His deep, royal blue eyes sent a shiver of excitement through her. She lifted her hand to her chest and gave him a discreet wave. Krispin beamed.

Jess's stomach flipped. An instant flash of. . .what? A dream, fantasy, prophecy? A vivid image of Krispin standing in the front of the church as she was walking down the center aisle to become his wife went through her mind's eye.

Could he be? Lord, is he the one?

"Good morning, Jess." Her father sat down beside her.

"Where's Mom?"

"She'll join us later. Jordan was up all night with Randi and the baby, so he asked Dena to fill in taking pictures for the testimonial part of the service."

Jess scanned the sanctuary. Over on the right side of the building, she saw her stepmother with a camera in hand and another around her neck.

"Dad, can Krispin join us for Sunday dinner?"

"Sure, except I believe Greg has planned a meal for his mentorees after the service."

"Okay, maybe another time."

"Are you two dating?"

"No!" she blurted out, perhaps too defensively.

Her father's beefy hand went over her own. "It's okay, sweetheart. I like him."

"I do, too. He's nothing like the man I first met."

"And that's a good thing." He squeezed her hand. "If Krispin asks you to join him for dinner, you're excused from the family meal."

Jess's smile brightened. She kissed her father on the cheek. "Thanks, Daddy."

"You're welcome."

The music started to play, and the worship leader stood up. Jess put all dreams and fantasies aside and concentrated on worshipping the Lord. Krispin floated into her mind only every other minute after that.

❧

Krispin's mouth went dry. He couldn't sing. He could barely stand up. *Lord, help me say the right words. My testimony needs to be about You, not me.*

Josiah's testimony came first. Krispin sat while he listened to Josiah confess his sins to his grandfather and the entire congregation.

"I'm afraid I have another confession." Josiah turned his gaze toward the area where Jess sat. "Jess, I'm the one who broke into your computer." The congregation gasped audibly.

"I needed some money. I thought I could get enough cash to hold me over for the summer through the co-op's financial records." The congregation rustled in their seats. "I wanted to help my kid, ya know?"

"Sheriff, I suppose that means another trial?" Josiah asked.

"More than likely," the sheriff replied.

"Jess, I'm truly sorry. I didn't mean to break your computer. I'll add that to my list of things to pay back."

Jess sat silently and nodded.

Josiah had grown up in the community. Krispin saw from the faces of those in the congregation how much of a disappointment Josiah had been to the folks who cared about him.

Josiah continued. "I don't know what else to say except, I'm sorry. Pastor Russell and Mr. Steadman have made me see how selfish I've been. Grandpa, I'm sorry. I don't know how, but I'm going to get the money back for you. Jesus has forgiven me. . .I know that. But I want to be the man you would be proud to call *Grandson* once again. I love you." Josiah's voice cracked, and he left the pulpit and sat down.

Krispin rubbed the sweat from his palms on to his slacks before he stood up. "Good morning," he said from behind the pulpit. "Most of you don't know me. My name is Krispin Black. I'm from New Hampshire, and I found the Lord here. Many of you know that Jessica Kearns ran over my kayak with her lobster boat several months back."

The congregation let out a nervous chuckle. Krispin reached out and held the pulpit to keep his knees from buckling.

"Besides saving my life that day, she put me on the path to the salvation of my soul. You see, I had no use for God. I wasn't even sure there was a God. Instead I saw Him as a helpful crutch for others to lean on to get them through life.

Well, you know what? He is. I finally came to realize I made a mess out of my own life. I found fortune and fame in my little corner of the world, but it left me cold and empty. My parents love me, but they loved themselves more. I was not a priority for them. Their own lives were more important to them, even while I was a small boy. I'm not saying that to blame them for how they raised me. But the way they expressed their love was very cold and distant, so I grew up with that same coldness.

"When I threatened Jess with the lawsuit, it was out of anger and from a way of life I'd been used to living. That's what you did in my world. You sued anyone for any inconvenience, including any you might have caused yourself. The truth is *I* was at fault that day. It wasn't Jess's fault. I wasn't paying attention and darted out from under the dock without looking.

"I know this sounds odd, but I'm grateful that Jess ran over me that day. I can see the Lord's hand was in it. You know, they say there are some hardheaded people in this world, and you have to hit them over the head with a two-by-four to knock any sense into them. But I'm especially hardheaded. God had to use an entire boat to get me to stop and reconsider my life choices."

The congregation gave a collective chuckle.

"I'm here today to proclaim I believe in God the Father, the Son, and the Holy Spirit. They live together as one, and Jesus is in my heart. I don't deserve Him or His love, but I'm thankful for it." Krispin let go of the pulpit and took his seat next to Josiah. The congregation burst into applause. Krispin bent his head in prayer. *Father, to You belongs all the glory. I'm the unworthy vessel. I'm not suited for this love, but I accept it. Thank You.*

The rest of the service was a blur. Krispin's mind stayed focused in prayer for God to be praised, not the people who were giving their testimonies.

❧

Jess couldn't wait for the service to end. She wanted to give

Krispin a great big hug. He deserved love. He deserved to be loved, and with God's grace, she would be the one to love him in the way he'd never known before. Her heart ached to be able to speak alone with him, but she knew the next few hours would be taken up with a brief reception after church and then the meal at the Steadmans'.

Jess stood with the congregation when instructed by the worship director. The room filled with the voices of people enjoying the presence of the Lord, His praises, and good friends and family. After the benediction Jess worked her way through the congregation to shake Krispin's hand, as well as those of the others who had given their testimonies, including Josiah Wood.

"Hey, Jess. I'm sorry," Josiah said.

"You're forgiven. And you didn't break the computer. It was part of an encryption program to shut it down when someone attempted to get in one too many times."

"Oh. Well, like I said, I'm sorry. I have no idea what the penalty will be for breaking and entering."

"Neither do I." Jess held back from telling Josiah that she wouldn't press charges. Frankly, she didn't quite feel he was completely repentant. There was a marked difference between his testimony and Krispin's. Then again, it could be her own emotions shading the events. In either case she'd have to pray about it and ask for some wise counsel on whether or not to pursue legal action.

She shook Josiah's hand and moved over to the one she most wanted to speak with. Instead of taking his hand after the person in front of her moved on, she gave Krispin a huge bear hug and whispered in his ear, "You did well and gave the Lord His due."

Krispin pulled out of her embrace but continued to hold her shoulders. Their eyes searched one another's for a moment. "Thanks, Jess. That means a lot."

"I wanted to invite you to the Sunday family dinner, but

Dad says you are probably going to the Steadmans'."

"Afraid so. Why don't I call you later?"

A line was gathering behind her. "Absolutely. Talk with you later." Jess moved toward Pastor Russell.

The afternoon passed with the speed of a slug crossing the sidewalk. Jess left her parents' house and returned to her own in time to receive Krispin's phone call.

"It's good to hear your voice, Krispin."

"Jess, I know this sounds horrible, but would you skip working with the youth tonight to go out with me?"

Jess giggled. "I don't have to skip out. The youth have a special event with another church's youth group so I didn't have to go. They had enough drivers and adult supervisors."

"Excellent. I mean. . ."

"Shh, I know what you mean. Please come over as soon as possible." Jess ached to share all that was in her heart, everything she hadn't spoken yesterday morning on the boat. For whatever reason she knew she loved Krispin and believed the vision she saw during church was God's way of saying it was okay to love him. She'd been afraid of her attraction for so long. Now she could allow it to grow and become what God intended for them as a couple.

Jess paced the living room as she waited for him to drive up. When she saw his Mustang turning in the drive, she ran out to greet him.

Krispin turned off the engine and slipped out of the car and into her arms. "Oh, Jess." He leaned down and kissed her.

Jess received his kiss and returned it, cradling his face in her hands.

Krispin broke away and held her. "I guess that answers the question."

I love you, Krispin. "And asks a whole lot more." Her heart beat wildly with love and fear.

"Definitely. Let's go inside. This town talks far too easily as it is."

Jess looped her arm around his elbow. He tensed for a moment, then relaxed. They walked to her house without a word spoken between them. She wondered about his hesitancy, then thought about what he said the day before, about his parents, about their lack of demonstrative love. *Was Krispin not so inclined?* "Are you afraid of physical touch because your parents weren't demonstrative?"

"No." He paused. "Jess, you have to know the whole truth about me before we can seriously consider a relationship. And once you do, you might not want to be anywhere near me."

fifteen

Krispin placed his hand over Jess's in the crook of his elbow. He didn't want to lose her, not now, not after everything he'd been through. But he knew she would have a serious problem being with a man like him, a man with a very stained past.

"Jess, my past—"

"Is in the past," Jess interrupted.

"Yes, I know. But you should know the extent of how bad it was."

"Krispin, you've already told me you were loose with women."

"Please, sit." Krispin released his grip and watched her gently settle on the sofa. He sat down beside her.

Jess sighed. "Krispin, we come from different backgrounds. But this morning I accepted once and for all that your faith is genuine. What happened back then were bad choices."

Krispin got up and paced. "You're not making this easy for me."

"Why? Because I forgive you? Am I supposed to ask how many? Am I supposed to ask what their names were? Is that really all that important at this time? Maybe later on, after we start dating and consider. . ."

"Marriage?" he supplied for her. "That's just it, Jess. I don't want to get involved with anyone if it isn't someone the Lord intends for me to marry. Look, I know the Lord forgives me. And I'm trying to forgive myself, but I know we can't enter a relationship without you knowing the truth about my past."

"All right. Tell me what you need to tell me."

Krispin sat down beside her once again. For the next fifteen minutes, he told her all he felt he should about his wrong choices and experiences, then concluded, "I'm sorry, Jess. I had no idea how God felt about marital love."

Jess closed her eyelids for a moment, then opened them slowly. "Krispin, I forgive you. You need to forgive yourself, and you should ask the Lord to forgive those other women for their part in the past sins."

"What are you suggesting?"

"Dad told me that he never felt truly forgiven for having gotten my bio-mom pregnant until he asked the Lord to forgive her. He'd taken the full responsibility for his actions upon himself. He forgot that Terry, my bio-mom, also chose to sin. Once he asked the Lord to forgive her for the part she played in their relationship, he finally felt really free from the past."

Krispin thought for a moment. He'd never asked the Lord to forgive the women he'd been involved with, only forgiveness for his part. *Is that why I'm still not feeling free from the past? Lord, forgive them.* "I never thought about that."

Jess smiled. "Now, let's change the subject. Tell me more about yourself, about your desires and dreams for the future. I want to get to know you better."

Krispin laughed. "You're incredible, Jessica Kearns. Do you have all night?"

"No, I have to work early tomorrow morning."

He popped up off the couch. "What time do you go to bed normally?"

"Nine."

He glanced at his wristwatch. "We have two hours. Are you hungry?"

"Nope. Just to know more about you."

"As I want to learn more about you. Let's do this: You ask a question, and I'll answer it. Then I ask the next question. Fair?"

"Sounds fair," she said. "What's your favorite color?"

"Brown."

"Brown? Why brown?"

"Nope, it's my turn." He smiled.

She turned and sat cross-legged on the couch and faced him. "Shoot."

"Well, I can tell by the decorations in your house that blue is your favorite color, which works well with your eyes, so I'm not going ask that. Let's see." He paused with a hum. "I got it. What was your favorite toy growing up?"

"Oh man, you're going to cringe at this one, but it was a large Tonka truck that my neighbors had in their backyard."

Krispin chuckled. "A real tomboy, huh?"

"Yes, plus that's a second question, so I get two. Why brown, and what was your favorite toy, besides a computer?"

"I like brown because it reminds me of wood, especially wood that's been stained. I guess it's because of the old library I'd spend so much of my time working in when I was a kid. As for a toy besides the computer, that would be my dirt bike. It was risky and adventurous. Plus my parents hated it. Mom feared I'd break a leg. Dad just hated the noise. I liked it, so they let me keep it. Obviously they didn't buy it for me. My grandfather did."

Jess laughed. "I had a few of those presents over the years. I think my CDs of teenybopper music just about killed my father. Of course Grandma said it was payback for all the heavy metal rock they had to endure when Dad was young."

They talked until nine. At last Krispin stood up. "It's time for me to go."

"Krispin, this has been nice. Thank you." Jess walked him to the door.

"The pleasure was all mine. Good night, Jess."

She leaned toward him. He reached out and combed her silky, honey-blond hair with his fingers. A knot the size of a CD lodged in the pit of his stomach. Jess reached up and brushed his face with her knuckles. A cord of warmth wrapped itself around his heart.

Jess touched his lips with the tip of her finger. "May I?" she whispered.

Unable to speak, he blinked his agreement. Her soft velvet lips gently pressed against his. His heart pounded in his chest—not because of wild excitement, but because it was a beautiful, chaste kiss. It said more to him than any other kiss he'd ever known. He knew at that very moment, Jessica Kearns loved him with a love so profound and pure it made him weak in the knees. *How? I don't. . .*

Jess pulled away. He opened his eyes. "Don't question God's forgiveness." She winked and stepped back. "Good night, Krispin."

Krispin slipped out the door and stood for a moment or two on the small landing that made up her stairway before his head cleared enough to remind him that he looked like a fool just standing on the woman's doorstep.

❧

Jess spent an hour in prayer before going to sleep, asking that the Lord would protect her thoughts and memories in the days to come. What Krispin had shared was limited, but she knew enough of the world to know what kind of a lifestyle he had led. In thinking back on the first time she had met him, it fit perfectly with her first impression. But he was a changed man, and he was sincere. And after the vision this morning in church, combined with the impact of their first two kisses, she knew beyond a shadow of doubt God was bringing them together. By His grace, she felt certain they would be married one day.

Thinking about that the next morning brought a smile to her face when she passed the spot in the harbor where she had run over Krispin and his kayak.

Her day flew by quickly. It was four in the afternoon when Krispin came into the co-op.

"Hey there, handsome. What brings you here?"

"You." His smile brightened up his eyes.

"What's up?"

"Nothing. I just thought I'd like to get a better feel for your passion with this co-op to understand you better."

"Sure. What would you like to know?"

"Nothing in particular. If you don't mind, I'd like to observe you while you work. I can check out your computers so you won't notice me."

Jess laughed. "Right. I haven't had any further trouble with the computers, but what Josiah said yesterday has me a little concerned."

"Everything's probably fine, but I'd like to check on the software I installed that recorded all the transactions on the computer."

The phone rang. Jess answered and waved for Krispin to go to work on the computer. The voice on the other end said, "I'd like two hundred one-and-a-half- to two-pound lobsters by Wednesday and another five hundred by Friday. Can you handle that order?"

Jess clicked a few keys on her keyboard. "Sure. What's your name? Have you ordered from us before?" She went on with her work and continued with the order. As she finished up with her call, Tom Wood, Josiah's grandfather, entered the co-op and engaged Krispin in a conversation.

"Hi, Mr. Wood," Jess interrupted. "What do you have for me today?"

"Not much." He handed her the inventory sheet from the holding tank.

She read the chicken scratch of the counter. "Fifty one-and-a-half- and twenty two-pounders. That's not too bad."

"Maybe not. I kept a couple for myself." The age spots on his hands were getting larger, she noticed. His hands shook a little.

"Can I get you a cup of coffee to warm your blood?" Krispin offered.

"That'd be right nice of you, thank you." Mr. Wood sat down. Jess went behind the desk and inputted his information.

"Are we still good for payment the end of the month?" Tom Wood asked. Krispin handed him a cup of coffee.

"If you're tight, I can give you an advance, Mr. Wood," Jess offered.

"I was hoping I could hire an attorney for Josiah, what with the new charges the sheriff is going to be adding on after his confession in church. I'm sorry he went after you, Jessica. You're a fine woman, and you've done a lot for us. I just don't understand that boy. Pastor is hopeful he's on the right trail this time. But I don't know. I've seen him repent before. Only time will tell."

Jess didn't know how to respond.

"Mr. Wood, if I were you, I'd hang on to your money as long as possible. It will take awhile for the sheriff to file the charges. Plus the public defender can take care of those."

"I probably should. I've given that boy the shirt off my back." He stopped from admitting anything further.

"Mr. Wood." Krispin put a loving hand on Mr. Wood's shoulder. "Wait on the Lord for this one."

"I suppose you're right. You really meant all you said yesterday, didn't you?"

"Yes, sir."

"Good, I hope you stick to it." Mr. Wood sipped his coffee and put the mug on the edge of Jess's desk. "I'll hold off until the end of the month."

"All right. Remember, if you need it, I can work something out."

"I'll be fine." Mr. Wood got up to leave.

Krispin called out to him as the old man ambled outside. "Hey, Mr. Wood. Wait up."

Jess watched from the store window to see a smile break across Mr. Wood's face. The two men shook hands and then Mr. Wood leaned into the cab of his truck. Krispin pulled out his wallet and gave him what looked to be a twenty-dollar bill. Jess laughed and went back to work. Krispin truly was a changed man. Who would pay twenty bucks for a lobster that he didn't even like to eat, except a man with a mission to do good for others. *Yes, Krispin Black, you and I are meant to be together.*

≈

Krispin put the large, three-pound lobster on the passenger seat of his Mustang and called Jess on the phone. "Hey, I'll be right back."

"What are you going to do with that lobster?"

"I thought about dumping it in the harbor. But then I remembered that Jordan loves these things with a passion, so I'm going to take it over to the Lamonts."

"Hang on; let me lock up and go with you."

"All right." Krispin closed the phone and got behind the wheel of his car. He gently grabbed the greenish blue crustacean and put him on the backseat of the car.

Jess bopped out of the co-op, her face lit with a contagious smile. "So, have you named him yet? You really shouldn't. You could get too attached."

"Ha-ha. I have no intentions of naming a lobster. I feel bad for that old man. He's been left with nothing. I think he needed money for more than hiring a lawyer for Josiah. I'd like to do something for him, but I don't know what."

"The church has a benevolent fund. If you know of someone in need, you tell the elders or pastor, and they give a love gift."

"That's not enough. This poor man lost his house because of Josiah."

"Not quite. Josiah doesn't know this, but between the church and the co-op, we managed to help Mr. Wood get a second mortgage on the house. As long as he keeps making his payments, he's got a place to live."

"And Josiah doesn't know this because. . ."

"No one is completely certain he's turned around yet. What's really scary is that if Josiah had gotten into the co-op's computer, he would have seen what we did to help his grandfather. He would have been a target again. Until there's more evidence of a changed life, no one wants Josiah to know."

"Makes sense. Still, I think Mr. Wood is hurting financially."

"Maybe. He probably spent the last of his cash on Josiah before his grandson went to prison. Mr. Wood is a good man, but he's got a huge blind spot when it comes to Josiah. You know what hit me in church was how different your testimony was compared with Josiah's. Josiah said he was sorry. He confessed to breaking into my house and computer, but he didn't give God any glory for the changes in his life. You, on the other hand, spoke little about what you'd done and more on what the Lord had done. It hit me then that Josiah still needs to put God first in his life. But at the time, I thought it was possibly me, unfairly misjudging his confession. Thinking about it now, I think maybe my impressions were right."

"Maybe, but it isn't our place to stand in judgment."

"No, but we are to be wise. And wisdom says to wait and see if Josiah is being sincere this time."

"On that, I totally agree."

"We're here." Krispin drove into Jordan and Randi's driveway. They were staying in the apartment above the photography studio. "Your stepmom owns this place, right?"

"Yup."

"I Googled her name. She's pretty famous," Krispin commented and reached behind him. "C'mon, Fred," he joked. "Uh-oh, I named him."

Jess let out a belly laugh. "What?"

"Fred."

"Well come on, Fred, you're going to make Jordan a happy man," Jess called out, walking up to the doorway of the apartment.

❧

Fred was a hit with Jordan. They stayed for a few minutes and played with the baby. Back in his car, Krispin asked, "Can I make you dinner?"

"Anytime," she quipped.

"Good. I'm enjoying the cooking."

"When I was in college, I was the take-out queen. As I told you before, Dena turned me on to cooking. I'm starting to like it, but not with the same enthusiasm as you have."

"We can learn together."

"I'd like that." Jess reached over and placed her hand on his. Krispin turned his hand and curled his fingers around hers. She brought his hand up to her lips and kissed the back of it. "I love you," she confessed.

He opened his mouth to blurt out the same when his cell phone rang the too familiar ring of his ex-partner in business. He answered. "Hi, Gary, what's up?"

"I need you. We have a huge emergency."

"What's the problem?"

"Something is wrong with the main components of several of your encryption codes. I know you're off somewhere finding yourself, but I really need you, man. The techs here have only been making the problem worse. I'll triple your pay. I need you for a month, possibly less."

"This isn't a good time, Gary."

"I don't care what it takes. Get here, and get here now. You gave your word you'd stand behind your product, and it is failing miserably. Get here by tomorrow morning. I'll hire a jet, if need be."

"All right. I'll be there in the morning."

"How about yesterday?"

"Okay, I can get there shortly after midnight. I'll need a room. I've sublet my apartment."

"Trust me, you won't have time to sleep. I'm setting you up in a secure and sealed-off room. You won't have access to any outside numbers."

"No way. I need an outside line, even if it is just the Internet."

"Separate unit?"

"Of course."

"Fine. I'll see you at midnight."

"What's the matter?" Jess knitted her brow. "You've got to go?"

"I'm afraid so, Jess. I don't want to, but I gave my word. I have to help."

"That's not a problem. I understand."

Krispin drove past his house and toward hers. "I'll drop you off. I'm sorry."

"Shh, don't you worry about it. I'll see you when you get back."

"Jess. . ." How could he tell her he might not be coming back for a month? With all the clarity that could come from a divine revelation, Krispin realized he might not know what he was going to do the rest of his life, but it would include Jessica Kearns. *If she'll have me.*

sixteen

Thirty days later, Krispin had still not returned. A weekly e-mail from him wasn't giving Jess a whole lot of satisfaction. She made arrangements with Myron Buefford to run the co-op in her absence while Dad took care of the lobstering. Jess drove up to the software company that Krispin had worked for, and even owned a portion of, before settling in Squabbin Bay. But had he really settled? He'd been gone for so long and—

She stopped the circular thinking that had plagued her for weeks.

Jess parked next to his Mustang and walked into the building. Its modern art and stainless steel statue in front glistened in the bright afternoon sun. The windows were three stories high. If a building could look high-tech, this one sure did.

She marched up to the receptionist.

"May I help you?" The woman had straight black hair pulled back in a bun. Her gray pinstripe suit declared all business.

"Yes, could you please tell me where I can find Krispin Black?"

"Do you have an appointment?"

"No."

"Well, I'm sorry, Mr. Black is not seeing any customers at this time."

"I'm not a customer." Jess narrowed her gaze. She wanted to say she was his fiancée, but nothing had ever been said about such a relationship, and she wouldn't presume it upon him. "Would you please just tell him that Jessica Kearns is here to see him?"

"Jessica Kearns." The woman wrote the name down, then popped her head up and scanned Jess from head to toe. "You're Jess?"

"Yes. Can I see him?"

"Uh, yeah. I guess so. Take the elevators to the third floor and take a right. His office is on your right. You can't miss it. It's the corner office."

"Thanks."

"You're welcome." She grinned as if knowing a secret. Whatever it was, Jess really didn't care. She wanted to see Krispin, and she was only a few feet away from him. *If this elevator would move.* Jess rapped her fingers on the stainless steel plate that housed the buttons for the various floors, having already punched in the number three. Impatient, she tapped it again. The doors closed. The floor jerked, then seemingly nothing until the door swooshed open on the third floor.

She walked down the hallway to the last office. Inside she found him with his back to the door. "Krispin?"

He jumped up and banged his knee on the keyboard. "Jess?" He ran up beside her. "Oh, honey, you're a sight for sore eyes."

Jess giggled and held on to him tightly. "So are you. I've missed you."

"And I, you. It's been horrible here. But I think I've finally created a new system."

"Krispin, I just want to hold you."

He held her close and kissed the top of her head. Joy filled her. "How long can you stay?"

"A couple days."

"I'll get you a suite."

"A suite?"

"Don't worry, it's a trade-off with the hotel. When we have customers we want to treat well, we put them in this suite. We manage the hotel's security software. It's a fair trade. The cost for me is that of renting a regular hotel room."

"All right. How long before you can take a break?" Jess asked and stepped out of Krispin's embrace.

He looked back at his computer, then back at her. He was pale and at least ten pounds thinner.

"Have you been eating?"

"A little. I've been shut up in a solitary room for days. I finally worked out the bugs and got through. It's an incredible program, Jess. The next level in encryption."

"I thought Gary asked you to fix a problem, not create a new program."

"I forget you don't understand all this stuff. Sorry. I fixed the problem. But what happened meant that all our other encryption programs that had those same components were vulnerable to this hacker. Replacing the software program with a totally different matrix seemed the logical course of action for the future. The stopgap I finished in a week. If the hacker's as good as I think he is, and if he's dedicated, he'll probably figure this one out in three months, possibly six. But that gives Gary's crew time to develop the new software they've been working on."

"I see."

Krispin chuckled. "I can tell by the glazed look in your eyes that I lost you. Suffice it to say, it's fixed, and the new and improved model should keep folks safe for a while."

"If you say so." Jess shook her head in disbelief. "You really are good at this stuff, aren't you?"

"He's the best," a deep male voice from behind her answered. She turned to see a man in his early thirties leaning against the doorway. "So you're Jess, huh?"

Krispin wrapped his arms around her. "The one and only."

She could feel Krispin's smile even if she couldn't see it.

"It's a pleasure to meet you. I'm Gary Ladd, owner of this company, and I'd be in your debt forever if you'd convince this man to come back to work for me. I've offered him fifty percent of the company, his own hours, and still he refuses."

Jess stilled in Krispin's arms. *He shouldn't be giving up his future, Lord.*

"I'm renting the suite for her."

"Not on your life. I'm paying. And I'd like you to take her out to the finest restaurant and put it on my credit card. Remember, you're unemployed. I'm not."

"But you're paying me three times the normal rate for the past month. I think I can afford to take my girlfriend out to dinner."

"Okay, I'll give that—you can afford it. Allow me to give you this gift."

"We'll think about it," Jess answered for him.

"That's all I ask." Gary turned his wrist. "Gotta run. It's a pleasure to meet you, Jess. Stop by again tomorrow. Perhaps we can chat some more." And he was off.

"Is he always like that?"

"Yes."

"Wow, he must take some getting used to."

"Most couldn't handle his abrupt changes in persona. By the time I was in the upper ranks of the company, I'd already seen how he operated, and it didn't bother me. He and I got along well. He truly does want me to come back. I'm not surprised, but I'm not really interested. I don't mind doing limited projects like this for him. But I don't want to have to be put in lockdown for weeks at a time. It's not healthy."

"No, you look horrible. I mean. . . " Jess stumbled over her words. "I mean, you don't look as healthy as when you left Squabbin Bay."

"I'm not. Besides not eating right, I've been working day and night to get this done, so I could get back to you. Jess, I've missed you so much. E-mails only made it more difficult to concentrate. That's why I didn't send you many. I'm sorry."

"Now that I'm here with you, everything is fine."

"Hang on a minute, and I'll take you to the hotel."

"I can find it."

Krispin chuckled. "I know you can. It's basically across the street. I want to get out of here, though, and I don't want you out of my sight."

Jess's heart jumped. "I'm all for that."

Within a couple minutes, they were locking his office and heading down the hallway, walking arm in arm. It was hard to believe how much she missed this man. Inside the elevator he leaned down and kissed her. Jess savored the moment and held on until they heard applause coming from behind them. She felt the heat rise in her cheeks. How'd they not noticed the doors had opened? She wanted to crawl under the floorboards and hide. Krispin wrapped a protective arm around her and escorted her out of the building.

❧

Inside her suite Krispin removed his shoes and gazed over the cart of food he'd ordered from room service. "Honey, do you want ice cream later?"

Jess came from behind the closed door of her bedroom. Her hair was damp from the shower. "What did you order?"

"A little of everything." He handed the waiter a substantial tip.

"Thank you, sir. Can I get you anything else?" The waiter smiled and waited for a response.

"No thanks. We'll call if we have any other need."

"Very good, sir. Ask for Ramone, and I'll take good care of you, sir." Krispin knew he could count on Ramone getting him and Jess anything they desired tonight. Krispin closed the door. Jess's beauty took his breath away.

As if reading his mind, she ran to him and wrapped her arms around his neck. "Kiss me before I faint," she begged.

She didn't have to ask twice. He kissed her with the fervor of all the love he had for her. It had been growing day by day for the past month. Whoever had said absence made the heart grow fonder certainly nailed it for the two of them.

"Marry me, Jess," he blurted out.

"Yes," she answered.

Then it hit him: what he had asked and what she had responded with. The realization struck him at the same time it dawned on her. An awkward silence filled the room. "I love you, Jess. I want you to be my wife, if you'll have me as a husband."

"I want to be your wife. But there's so much left unsaid between us. So much we don't know about one another yet."

"Agreed. How do we approach this situation now?"

"We could marry ASAP. Dad told me to be very careful and guard my heart so as not to be too vulnerable while we're alone together."

Krispin laughed. "I can see you paid attention."

She jabbed him in the ribs. "Let's eat. We'll figure this out as we go along."

"Excellent idea."

Jess took the hotel's white china plate and sampled the different cheeses and fruit, then placed the steak with mushrooms and onions on her dish. Krispin did the same and added a bowl of cream of asparagus soup.

"Be careful not to eat too much. How many meals did you skip?"

"Way too many. You look great, though."

"Thanks. The shower helped." She sat down on the sofa and put the plate of food on the coffee table. "Krispin, why didn't you call me?"

"I was afraid if I heard your voice I wouldn't be able to concentrate on the project. I was trying desperately to finish it so I could get home to you. I told Gary if I didn't finish it in two more days, I was leaving for a visit. I'm so glad to see you."

"Krispin, we should get married, just not tonight."

"Agreed. Don't you need to get blood tests or something first?"

"Not anymore. But you do need a marriage license, and we

have to pick that up at the town hall."

"We could find a minister to marry us tomorrow," Krispin hinted.

"And who's going to tell my father we eloped?"

"I get your point. What if we call them and ask them to join us?"

Jess took a forkful of steak and chewed it thoroughly before she spoke. "I think I know why you're so good at writing software—you stick to it. Which will be a good thing in marriage. However, I've always dreamed of getting married in Squabbin Bay at the church, the white gown, walking down the aisle, a flower girl, the whole bit."

Krispin swallowed the chunk of apple he'd just bitten off. "How much time do you need?"

"Honey, there's a lot of work at the co-op right now. I can't see myself getting married until next June."

"June? That's like seven months away."

"Exactly."

Krispin sobered. "If you want to wait seven months, I think I'll take a couple of jobs Gary offered me. They will take a couple of months."

"Why?"

Krispin swallowed hard. "Jess, that's a long time to be close to you without something else to occupy my thoughts."

"Yes, so? Oh!" Her eyes widened. "Okay. What about you helping me at the co-op?"

"Doing what?"

"There's a ton of things. I know we could be better organized. The software we have doesn't fully integrate all the information to the various areas I need to retrieve it, so I'm inputting the same information two or three times a day."

"I can handle that. So could we get married in November? If I take that on?"

"That's next month."

Okay, I'm missing something here. He thought of a movie

he'd seen about what women want and remembered a line about proms being all about the dress. "Jess, how much time do you need to get the dress, set up the wedding the way you'd like? I want you to have the wedding you've always dreamed about."

Jess giggled. "Daddy would die. He'd have to work a third job to pay for it."

"Seriously, Jess, what do you want? I'll do whatever it takes to make that day special for you. And I can pay for it. Your father doesn't have to."

There was a long pause. "You know what? I'm not thinking about this right. You're willing to give me everything I want, and I haven't offered to give you anything you want. What do you want, Krispin?"

"Only one thing: to be your husband. I don't care how the process happens. I just want to do it right."

"What about your parents?"

"I'll find them and let them know. I'm pretty sure they'll come, if they can be reached." Krispin resumed eating. So did Jess.

After a few minutes, she said, "How about if we get married a week before Thanksgiving?"

"Seriously?"

"Yeah. I know the photographer, so that's not a problem. We can have it at the church, and we can have it catered or have folks bring potluck."

Krispin wiped his mouth with the linen napkin. "We'll cater."

"How many invitations for your friends from here?"

"Probably no more than a dozen, if that. If you've noticed, no one came out to visit with me."

"Do you think Gary would come?"

"If he can still do business on the side."

"He can't be that bad, can he?"

"Just about. But he'll come, and he'll bring his wife."

"He's married?"

"Yeah. I never could figure how he managed to keep a wife, but he does, somehow. Are you sure, Jess?"

"Yes, I'm sure. Now hurry up and finish your dinner. I want to go out and spend some time in your city."

"Okay. What about careers, Jess? Are you willing to leave Squabbin Bay, lobstering, and the co-op if some opportunity came up for me to work somewhere else?"

seventeen

Jess fought all night with the question Krispin had asked her before they went out. She avoided the answer, saying something lame like she'd deal with it when the time came. But the time was now. Krispin had excellent opportunities to stay with this company. He meant a lot to them and their future. How could she possibly pull him away from all of that?

She'd gone to work with him in the morning in order to retrieve her car. Today she sat in the suite, bored and alone. She thought about going shopping, but that wasn't the answer. This was what life would be like with Krispin. He'd go to work, she'd stay home and do what? Raise babies?

Jess wanted children, but that wasn't her only goal in life. She had a business degree and would like to continue using it. *I wonder if I could find a job in this company? But what about the co-op? I can't desert them now. Perhaps in a year, when we're really established, but right now seems too soon, Lord. What should we do?*

She picked up her cell phone and called her stepmother. "Mom, it's Jess. I need some help."

"What's the matter, Jess? Are you all right? Krispin didn't—"

"Oh, no, nothing like that. He asked me to marry him."

"Congratulations! Wait—are you happy about that?"

"Yes, but, oh—I don't know. He's got great career opportunities here. They love him, and he's a valuable member of their staff, Mom. I just don't feel like I can take him away from this. And then there is the co-op. I can't leave it now. It's too fragile."

"I see. You know, Jess, your father and I had similar

157

problems before we got married. I had a career that took me all over the world. He wanted to stay in Squabbin Bay. In the end, we worked it out. If Krispin is the right man, it will work out."

Jess sighed. "I know. We talked about eloping but figured Dad would have my head. Plus, I still would like to get married in the church."

Dena let out a nervous chuckle. "Sweetheart, I know the pain of trying to decide. Unfortunately, I can't answer this question for you. You and Krispin have to work this out."

"Yeah, I suppose so. It's just that I was hoping you could tell me what to do."

"I can tell you what not to do. And eloping would fit in there somewhere, only because your father would like to attend and give his blessings on his little girl's wedding, not to mention the rest of us." Dena paused. "Jess, I truly understand the agony you're going through right now. But try to be patient and wait on the Lord."

"Mom, here's the thing. Krispin doesn't want to wait a long time. He's more concerned about not sinning. What do you think of the weekend before Thanksgiving?"

"I understand. Your father and I didn't wait a long time either. But—"

"I know, you were older. I had a vision the Sunday morning that Krispin gave his testimony. I saw us getting married in the church."

"Honey, I don't doubt that you love Krispin or that he loves you. I don't even doubt that the Lord is behind this. What concerns me is the time you haven't had together to become friends. It's that friendship that will get you through the ups and downs of life. And marriage is hard work. I love your dad with all my heart, but there are adjustments we both have to go through."

"I know what you're saying is right. I just don't want to hinder Krispin's career."

"That's Krispin's choice, as it is your choice about the co-op. You say it is at a critical time, but the fact of the matter is the co-op can move on without you, if you let it go. I'm not saying it is the right thing to do, I'm just remembering back to my own decision-making process. Letting jobs be done by others rather than myself was a hard thing to allow. You created a good co-op. You could let someone do the daily running of the business and still stay on the board to help oversee the growth of the company, couldn't you?"

"Yeah, I suppose I could. But who could do my job?"

Dena laughed. "I don't know. I do know one thing: It won't be your father."

Jess joined her stepmom in the humor of that statement. Time was precious to her parents, and she knew it. "Thanks, Mom."

"You're welcome. Please tell me I can tell your father the news."

"Nope, I'll do it. Right now."

"Great, 'cause I don't think I could have kept this a secret."

They ended the conversation, and Jess called her father on his cell phone. He didn't pick up, so she left him a message to call Dena for the news. Then she reached for her purse and headed out of the suite to take in some of the sights of the city.

❧

"Krispin, this is incredible."

"I'm pleased, but you and I both know it won't take long before someone is able to crack it. In my opinion you need to get some of the younger guys working with this right away so they can take it to the next level."

"I understand. Krisp, please reconsider and come back to work for us."

"I can't. It's not a healthy environment for me."

"True, you don't look so hot. Okay, what about this? I keep you on retainer, and you work from wherever you are."

"I'll think about it. I'm not like you, Gary. I can't separate my work and my personal life. I get too obsessed with it. I couldn't do that to Jess. I honestly don't understand how you manage to have a successful marriage."

"That's because she and I run in very different circles. She has her work; I have mine. You notice we don't have children. Neither one of us wants to give up the time it would take to raise kids. It works for us."

"I know Jess would like to have children one day—not right away, but one day. She's really quite an intelligent businesswoman. She put together—"

"The co-op, yeah, you told me. And what's that encryption program you put on her server?"

"You checked?"

"Of course. I always check into my competition, and frankly, Jessica Kearns is my competition. However, I can see I won't win against her. Promise me you'll seriously consider the idea of going on retainer and working remotely."

"We'd have to talk about it further. And I'd limit myself to only a couple projects a year."

"You can't live on that, can you?"

"It would be tight. However, I'll probably agree to a certain percentage of the profit from the program sales."

Gary shook his head in disbelief. "You'll do all right. You're still a wise businessman."

"I learned from the best." Krispin winked. "Gary, I know you think I've gotten all holy and stuff, and perhaps you're right. But trust me, I have more peace now than I've ever had in my entire life. And at the same time, I have more issues with no answers or quick resolutions. It's weird, but Jesus really does help."

"If you say so. Look, I don't mean to brush you off since you started talking religion again, but I do have an appointment in three minutes. Thanks for this. I don't know how to pay you back for it."

Krispin chuckled. "You will. Here's my bill." Krispin tossed an invoice over to him.

Gary's eyes bulged. "Wow, that's triple?"

"All except the percentage of sales for this product. That's at the same standard I used to earn."

"I guess you can only work on two or three projects a year."

Krispin smiled. "Thanks, Gary."

Gary initialed the invoice and handed it back. "You're worth it, man. Call me once in a while."

"You'll be getting a wedding invitation."

"Louise and I will be there."

"Great. God bless." Krispin walked out of Gary's office a new man. It wasn't the same as when he'd left the company all those many months ago. Instead he was standing the victor, knowing he was walking the right path in the right direction—and into the arms of the woman he loved. Life couldn't get any better than this.

He pulled out his cell phone and called his parents. The service said they were out of communications range. He left a message, telling them he'd be getting married in November and asking them to return the call as soon as they could.

Somehow it didn't surprise him that they weren't available to hear the news. *Father, try to reach my parents. They're good people, just self-absorbed. Help me deal with them.*

Krispin walked to accounting and waited for them to process the check. Ruthie Martin stood at the printer, waiting for it to be printed. "Mr. Black, I hear you're getting married."

"Yes, Ruthie, I am."

"Congratulations. Is it this woman from Maine that everyone's been talking about?"

"Yes."

Ruthie smiled and retrieved the check. "Wow! I'm sorry, what you're paid is none of my business."

"That's all right." Krispin took the proffered check and folded it in half.

"Will you be coming back to the company? Everyone's been wondering."

"No, I'll probably do some side jobs and come in for emergencies. But let's hope there aren't any more emergencies."

"Yeah. Everyone talked about you being here, but no one really saw all that much of you. You came to work before anyone else, and you left after everyone else."

Krispin didn't want to tell her of the numerous nights he never left. "Good-bye, Ruthie."

"Good-bye, Mr. Black." Ruthie sat back down at her console and began typing. Krispin walked out and looked back at the tall office building they had built five years earlier. Back then he had been a junior-level partner. He knew his programs were the backbone for the early growth of the company, but it would take a team of programmers to bring the company further up the software chain to become the best in the world for encryption.

A slow smile eased up the corners of his mouth. It no longer mattered to him if he was the best in the world. He was content to be the best man he could be for the Lord and for Jessica. He flipped open his phone and called her. "Hey, where are you? I'm done."

The lilt of Jess's laughter felt like warm honey on a sore throat. "You won't believe this, but I'm at a bridal shop."

"Oh, really? Did you find anything you like?"

"Uh-huh. I'm standing in front of the mirrors with it on."

A rush of emotions hit Krispin all at once. He could picture her standing in front of three mirrors dressed in white. "Jess, I love you."

"I love you, too, Krispin. The saleswoman is here. I'll call you in a couple minutes."

"Sure. I'm heading to the hotel suite."

"Let's meet for lunch."

"Okay. Go to Richard's Bistro—it's on Lowell Street—say in thirty minutes?"

"Make it forty-five."

Krispin chuckled. "No problem. See you there." He drove down to Lowell Street and parked outside a jewelry store. Glancing at his watch, he made a quick detour inside. Finding mostly secondhand jewelry, he decided to look but not purchase. The thought of giving Jess a "used" engagement ring didn't set well. It would be one thing if it were a family heirloom, but this would never do.

"Can I help you, sir?"

"I was looking for an engagement ring, but I'm looking for something new."

"I understand. We have a fine variety of rings. What some of my customers have done is purchase the ring here and have the stones reset in a new setting."

"Hmm." Krispin scanned the glass counter. "Why is this diamond almost yellow?"

"That's a rare type of diamond. Be warned of the imitations out there. . .stones that have been chemically altered."

"How can you tell the difference?"

"You can't, but an honest jeweler can. There are also pink diamonds."

"May I see the yellow diamond ring?"

"Sure." The gentleman took a key ring from his pocket and opened the cabinet. A small, white price tag dangled from the ring. Krispin glanced at it, then refocused his gaze. "Is that the correct price?"

"Yes. It's actually a steal. Brand-new can run from five to forty thousand for that carat. The clarity of the stones accounts for the higher figure."

Krispin handed the diamond back. The idea of a beautiful ring for a beautiful woman thrilled him. The idea of her fishing with a ring of such great value seemed foolish. "What do regular diamonds go for?" Krispin could feel the sweat beading on his forehead. Marriage was going to cost him big-time.

❧

Jess sat down beside Krispin at the restaurant. It had taken her the full forty-five minutes to dress and worm her way out of the store. The saleswoman unsuccessfully tried to convince her that seven thousand dollars was appropriate for a woman like her to spend on a wedding gown. *Not!*

"What's the matter?" Krispin asked as she settled into the chair.

"Nothing."

"Did you like the dress?"

Jess sighed. "Yes, but there's no way I'm going to spend seven thousand on a dress. I'd rather save it for something more important."

"Seven isn't too bad. You should have seen a price tag I saw earlier. Did you know that yellow diamonds could cost forty thousand?"

"Please tell me you didn't spend that! Did you?"

"No. I'm far more practical than that. It was a pretty ring, but not that pretty."

"Phew."

Krispin reached over and held her hand. "Jess, let's pray."

Jess nodded. And Krispin began. "Father, guide us in the decisions we're going to be making over the next few days. Help us to make the right choices. I want to give Jess the kind of wedding she has dreamed of, but help us be practical in choosing what, when, and how much."

"Father," Jess added, "please help us to be in agreement with one another and not to be sidetracked by what others think or believe is acceptable for a marriage ceremony. Amen."

"Amen." Krispin's rich baritone voice spiraled down to the depths of her being. She could feel herself calming.

"So what is the normal price for a wedding gown?" he asked. "I already have a tux, so that isn't a problem."

"You own your own tux?"

"Yeah, it seemed practical at the time. I had several events where I needed to rent one, so I simply purchased it. Anyway, what kind of a dress do you want?"

"I loved the one I had on. It had all sorts of fancy beading and just sparkled wonderfully in the lights. I could see myself in it. But then again, it seemed too, oh, I don't know, rich for my taste. I'm basically a jeans and sweater type of gal. Don't get me wrong, I like nice clothes, and I love the feel of fine silk against my skin but—"

Krispin held up his hand. "I understand. One of the reasons I didn't buy the ring was that I just couldn't picture the ring on your finger while your hand was diving into that chum bucket."

Jess laughed. "I wear gloves."

"I know, but still, it wasn't the kind of jewelry you would wear on the job. Personally, I'm looking for a simple gold band that tells the world I'm married, and that's it. I'm not interested in impressing anyone. I do want to get you an engagement ring, but I want to be practical about it. What would you feel comfortable wearing every day?"

"Probably just a solitaire. . .nothing huge, just a simple-cut ring."

"Yeah, that's what I was picturing, too. Good, we have similar tastes."

Jess squeezed his hand. "I told Mom. I couldn't reach Dad."

"I called my parents, as well, but could only leave word on their answering service."

"Krispin, I've been thinking. Are we making the right decision? I mean. . ." *What do I mean?* "I can see us getting married one day, and I understand your desire to marry quickly, but. . ."

"You need more time?" He rubbed the top of her hand with the ball of his thumb.

"Yes. . .no. . .maybe. . .I don't know. All I do know is that it isn't right for you not to work in the place where you shine.

As for me, I'm hesitant to leave Squabbin Bay, not because of the area, but because of the co-op."

"Jess, I have no intention of moving back into the rat race that I was once in to help develop this company. I can, and probably will, develop more software for them. However, I've got to learn how to stop working." He leaned in closer. "Here's the thing. I'm obsessive when it comes to developing new programs. I don't break away as often as I should. I couldn't do that to you."

"So what are you saying?"

Krispin closed the few inches between them and kissed Jess's forehead.

"May I take your order now?" the waiter interrupted.

Jess pulled away. She'd been so focused she'd forgotten their surroundings. Krispin ordered a cold steak salad for both of them. After the waiter left, he said, "I'm saying I don't have to work for anyone except myself. I can develop the software and sell it to Gary. He'll package and sell the programs. I don't want the headache of business. I simply want to be creative and write the programs."

Jess smiled. "Mom suggested I should start letting other people work for the co-op."

"Is that what you want to do?"

"No. I like working. I like planning and moving the co-op forward."

Krispin laughed. "The very things I really don't like in the business world."

"Yeah, I guess we're opposites there."

"Look, Jess, I'll wait as long as you want to get married. I love you, and I can't believe God is allowing me to find a wife. I simply am not worthy of it. You deserve better."

She laid a finger to his soft, warm lips. "Shh, we've been over this. You're suited for love just as much as everyone else. I love you, Krispin, and I love the man you have become."

"I'm glad I'm not the man you first met. But, Jess, there

are parts of me that are still that man. I'm not perfect. I've changed but—"

"You're perfect for me," Jess finished his statement.

"You know how to tickle my ears. So are we still on for the Saturday before Thanksgiving?"

"Yes. Where do you want to go for our honeymoon?"

"Hmm, I haven't thought that far. Where do you want to go?"

"I love camping, kayaking, and all those outdoor things, but I'd really love to go to Italy—to Venice. I've never been there, and a city on water intrigues me."

"Venice it is. Do you have a passport?"

"Yeah, Mom insisted on it, saying she'd like for all of us to travel together sometime."

Krispin sat back. The waiter approached and placed their steak salads down in front of them, then disappeared. He picked up his fork, then laid it back on the table. "Let's pray."

Jess slipped her fingers into the palm of his hand. She loved the feel of his touch. She could see herself getting old and gray and still cherishing holding this man's hand. The Lord had answered her prayer and brought the perfect man into her life. A man with an unworthy past but standing on the promises of God, washed in the blood, and fearfully and wonderfully made to be her life partner. *Thank You, Jesus.*

epilogue

Jess slipped her hand into Krispin's, then turned to her father. He lifted the veil and kissed her on the cheek. "I love you, sweetheart."

"I love you, too, Daddy."

Krispin squeezed her hand and gave Wayne a wink. Pastor Russell continued with the wedding service. "Dearly beloved, we are gathered here today. . . ."

Her eyes met Krispin's. The confessions of love and fidelity were spoken with such truth and honesty Jess had no doubt this man would keep his word to her and to God. Her love for Krispin deepened as she professed her love to him.

"Krispin, you may kiss your bride." Pastor Russell smiled.

Krispin cradled her head in his hands. "I love you, Jess."

"I love you, too."

Their lips met. A deep warmth of excitement, passion, and completeness filled out the kiss. Oh yes, she was one with this man and would be for the rest of her life.

Slowly the sounds of the cheers and clapping from those watching penetrated their senses, and Krispin pulled away. His fingers slid down her arms and entwined hers. They turned and met the congregation.

"May I present to you for the first time, Mr. and Mrs. Krispin Black."

Jess's smile filled her face. Krispin's did the same.

The old pipe organ cranked out the traditional wedding recessional, and Krispin led her down the aisle, past his parents, past hers. In the row behind her father and stepmother was her bio-mom, Terry, with her husband and children. Jess smiled. Terry actually seemed comfortable being there.

Krispin pulled Jess into his embrace once they stepped into the foyer. "I love you, Mrs. Black."

"I love you, too."

"What did your mom say about her matron of honor present?"

"She and Dad were floored. I can't believe you worked it out for them to join us the second week in Italy."

"Well, you said your father wanted to travel more, and I know Dena's been there before, so she'll be a great tour guide."

"Honey, that isn't why you invited them, is it?"

"No, it isn't. But I love the togetherness of your family."

"I know, and that's what I told them. They're excited and will be joining us."

"Great. Besides, your stepbrother, Chad, got us a fantastic rate. Oh, by the way, he and his family will be joining us, as well."

"What?" Jess's knees felt weak.

"I rented a large villa for the second week. There are six bedrooms, so I figured we had room to invite the rest of the family to join us. I know that Amber and David would never be able to afford a trip like this, and neither would pastor, so I figured with the rate Chad was able to get, we could afford to bring the entire clan over with us."

"You're kidding!"

People were gathering to shake their hands and congratulate them. "Nope. I figured it would be fun to have a family Thanksgiving in Italy."

"Do Mom and Dad know?"

"Probably by now. I had the family keep it a surprise from you and your parents. I had to check with them to see if they could arrange their schedules to join us. It took some work, but they'll all be able to come."

"Just how much money did you make last month?"

Krispin leaned over and whispered in her ear. Jess's eyes

bulged. "You're kidding!" she said again.

"Nope."

"So you could have afforded that forty-thousand-dollar ring?"

"Yup. But this trip is better than that ring, right?"

Jess started to giggle. She giggled all during the receiving line. Not only was Krispin Black suited for love, he was the giver of love to others. As they walked back into the church for the wedding photos, she said, "You're nuts, you know."

"Absolutely. Nuts about you and nuts about a forgiving God who has blessed me beyond all I could ever hope for."

"I love you."

"I love you, too." They stood arm in arm and posed for the cameras. Jess's heart swelled yet again with love for this incredible man. And for an incredible God who would, and could, take away all the hardness of the world and make vessels suitable for His love for others.

A Letter To Our Readers

Dear Reader:

In order that we might better contribute to your reading enjoyment, we would appreciate your taking a few minutes to respond to the following questions. We welcome your comments and read each form and letter we receive. When completed, please return to the following:

Fiction Editor
Heartsong Presents
PO Box 719
Uhrichsville, Ohio 44683

1. Did you enjoy reading *Suited for Love* by Lynn A. Coleman?
   ❏ Very much! I would like to see more books by this author!
   ❏ Moderately. I would have enjoyed it more if

   _____
   _____
   _____

2. Are you a member of **Heartsong Presents**? ❏ Yes ❏ No
   If no, where did you purchase this book? _____
   _____

3. How would you rate, on a scale from 1 (poor) to 5 (superior), the cover design? _____

4. On a scale from 1 (poor) to 10 (superior), please rate the following elements.

   ____ Heroine   ____ Plot
   ____ Hero   ____ Inspirational theme
   ____ Setting   ____ Secondary characters

5. These characters were special because? _____

_____

_____

6. How has this book inspired your life? _____

_____

_____

7. What settings would you like to see covered in future
   Heartsong Presents books? _____

_____

_____

8. What are some inspirational themes you would like to see
   treated in future books? _____

_____

_____

9. Would you be interested in reading other **Heartsong
   Presents** titles? ❏ Yes ❏ No

10. Please check your age range:
    ❏ Under 18   ❏ 18-24
    ❏ 25-34   ❏ 35-45
    ❏ 46-55   ❏ Over 55

Name _____

Occupation _____

Address _____

City, State, Zip _____

Heartng

CONTEMPORARY ROMANCE IS CHEAPER BY THE DOZEN!

Any 12 Heartsong Presents titles for only $27.00*

Buy any assortment of twelve *Heartsong Presents* titles and save 25% off the already discounted price of $2.97 each!

*plus $3.00 shipping and handling per order and sales tax where applicable. If outside the U.S. please call 740-922-7280 for shipping charges.

HEARTSONG PRESENTS TITLES AVAILABLE NOW:

___HP541 *The Summer Girl*, A. Boeshaar
___HP545 *Love Is Patient*, C. M. Hake
___HP546 *Love Is Kind*, J. Livingston
___HP549 *Patchwork and Politics*, C. Lynxwiler
___HP550 *Woodhaven Acres*, B. Etchison
___HP553 *Bay Island*, B. Loughner
___HP554 *A Donut a Day*, G. Sattler
___HP557 *If You Please*, T. Davis
___HP558 *A Fairy Tale Romance*, M. Panagiotopoulos
___HP561 *Ton's Vow*, K. Cornelius
___HP562 *Family Ties*, J. L. Barton
___HP565 *An Unbreakable Hope*, K. Billerbeck
___HP566 *The Baby Quilt*, J. Livingston
___HP569 *Ageless Love*, L. Bliss
___HP570 *Beguiling Masquerade*, C. G. Page
___HP573 *In a Land Far Far Away*, M. Panagiotopoulos
___HP574 *Lambert's Pride*, L. A. Coleman and R. Hauck
___HP577 *Anita's Fortune*, K. Cornelius
___HP578 *The Birthday Wish*, J. Livingston
___HP581 *Love Online*, K. Billerbeck
___HP582 *The Long Ride Home*, A. Boeshaar
___HP585 *Compassion's Charm*, D. Mills
___HP586 *A Single Rose*, P. Griffin
___HP589 *Changing Seasons*, C. Reece and J. Reece-Demarco
___HP590 *Secret Admirer*, G. Sattler
___HP593 *Angel Incognito*, J. Thompson
___HP594 *Out on a Limb*, G. Gaymer Martin
___HP597 *Let My Heart Go*, B. Huston
___HP598 *More Than Friends*, T. H. Murray
___HP601 *Timing is Everything*, T. V. Bateman
___HP602 *Dandelion Bride*, J. Livingston
___HP605 *Picture Imperfect*, N. J. Farrier
___HP606 *Mary's Choice*, Kay Cornelius
___HP609 *Through the Fire*, C. Lynxwiler
___HP613 *Chorus of One*, J. Thompson

___HP614 *Forever in My Heart*, L. Ford
___HP617 *Run Fast, My Love*, P. Griffin
___HP618 *One Last Christmas*, J. Livingston
___HP621 *Forever Friends*, T. H. Murray
___HP622 *Time Will Tell*, L. Bliss
___HP625 *Love's Image*, D. Mayne
___HP626 *Down From the Cross*, J. Livingston
___HP629 *Look to the Heart*, T. Fowler
___HP630 *The Flat Marriage Fix*, K. Hayse
___HP633 *Longing for Home*, C. Lynxwiler
___HP634 *The Child Is Mine*, M. Colvin
___HP637 *Mother's Day*, J. Livingston
___HP638 *Real Treasure*, T. Davis
___HP641 *The Pastor's Assignment*, K. O'Brien
___HP642 *What's Cooking*, G. Sattler
___HP645 *The Hunt for Home*, G. Aiken
___HP649 *4th of July*, J. Livingston
___HP650 *Romanian Rhapsody*, D. Franklin
___HP653 *Lakeside*, M. Davis
___HP654 *Alaska Summer*, M. H. Flinkman
___HP657 *Love Worth Finding*, C. M. Hake
___HP658 *Love Worth Keeping*, J. Livingston
___HP661 *Lambert's Code*, R. Hauck
___HP665 *Bah Humbug, Mrs. Scrooge*, J. Livingston
___HP666 *Sweet Charity*, J. Thompson
___HP669 *The Island*, M. Davis
___HP670 *Miss Menace*, N. Lavo
___HP673 *Flash Flood*, D. Mills
___HP677 *Banking on Love*, J. Thompson
___HP678 *Lambert's Peace*, R. Hauck
___HP681 *The Wish*, L. Bliss
___HP682 *The Grand Hotel*, M. Davis
___HP685 *Thunder Bay*, B. Loughner
___HP686 *Always a Bridesmaid*, A. Boeshaar
___HP689 *Unforgettable*, J. L. Barton
___HP690 *Heritage*, M. Davis
___HP693 *Dear John*, K. V. Sawyer
___HP694 *Riches of the Heart*, T. Davis

(If ordering from this page, please remember to include it with the order form.)

Presents